ARTIFICIAL INTRIGUES

TEN SHORT STORIES OF AI AND CRIME

NIDHI ARORA

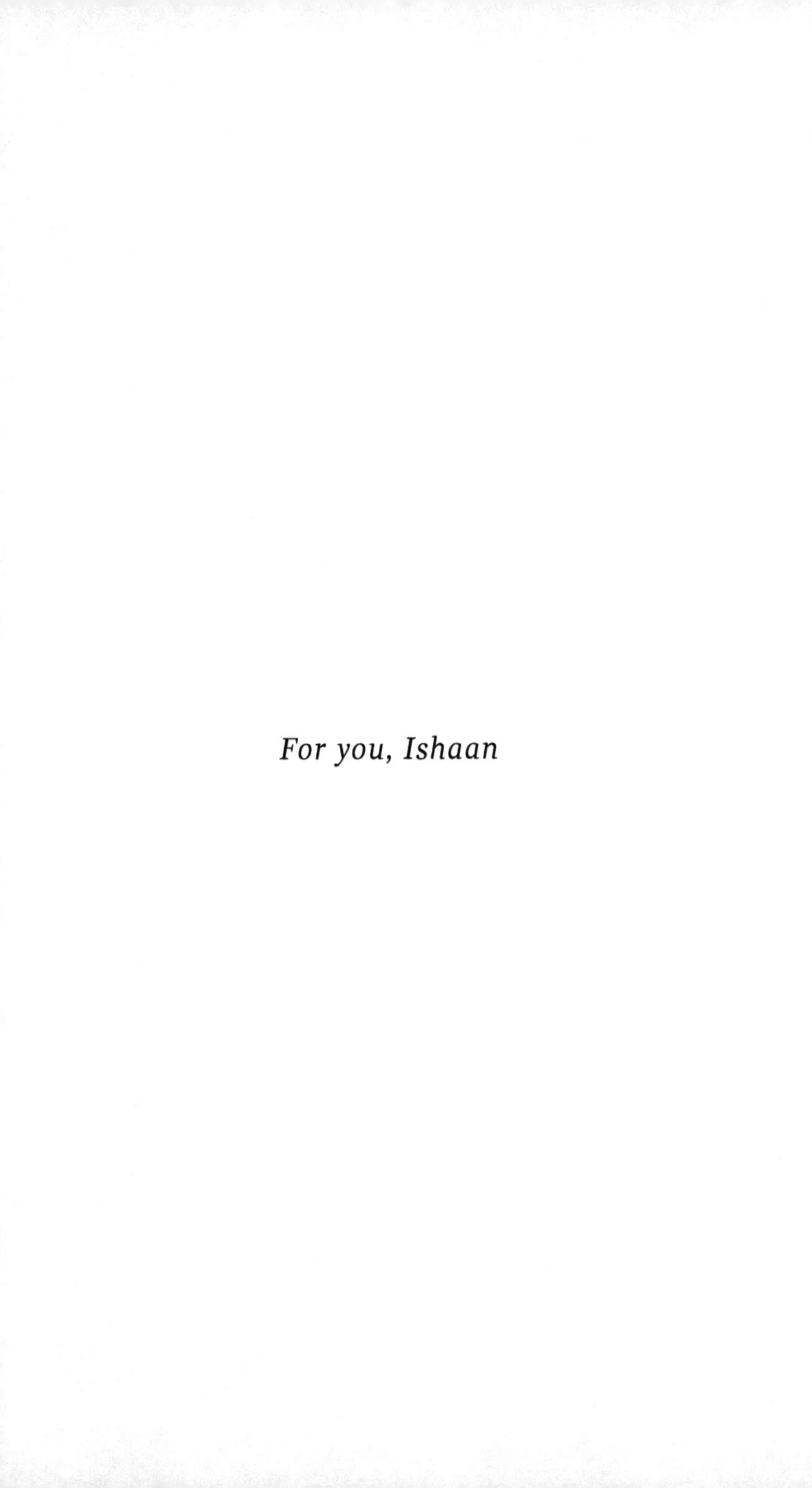

For you, Ishaan

Contents

About This Book   vii

Foreword   ix

Preface   xi

Acknowledgements   xiii

1. The Will Of Roshan Dalal   1

2. Malti Marg   14

3. Maja Ni Life   27

4. The Kidnapping Story   45

5. Brtdr.xyz   56

6. The Ambria Trialogue   72

7. Sis Code   92

8. 8. The Diary Of Amit Sharma – II   99

9. The Patel Takeover   116

10. Anika   125

Epilogue   137

About This Book

"The best part of Nidhi's stories is that they incorporate technology into the criminal acts, especially how people use or misuse it for sinister purposes. The other part is that she does not throw around technicalities and jargons but simplifies them through her writing style. I am sure that readers will be glued to the stories and enjoy reading them without distraction. I wish her every success with this and future books!"

Amal Gupta

Digital enthusiast by profession and sportsman by passion

"As we discuss AI and Gen AI, one application that remains largely unaddressed is crime and crime prevention. I thoroughly enjoyed reading these cases. Each one was an eye-opener. But what was most amazing was that in at least two cases, the author mentions that the case has already also happened in real life. Scary! Therefore, a must-read book.

I would call this book a thriller. The thrill is in figuring out which case will go from fictional to real next."

- Deshant Kaila

Global Leader in the GCC/Tech space

Foreword

Every day technology advances and makes our lives easier. It also makes crime easier. This is particularly true in the age of AI, when what is real and what is fake is becoming difficult to decipher. And it seems like creativity in execution of crime has reached an all-time peak.

But every such bit of news is fodder for Nidhi Arora's imagination. She can spin an intriguing story predicting what kind of crimes can take place in the future! I say this because one story in this book has this disclaimer - the modus operandi she imagined has been used by real criminals.

Hmm. It's difficult to say whether art imitates life or vice versa. Wonder whether Nidhi's short stories will soon be recommended reading for budding scamsters! But on a serious note, it takes a unique kind of talent to write gripping stories about cutting edge crime.

Of course, technology also helps in solving crime in ways that would have been impossible. So, there's hope yet. The battle of good vs evil is an eternal one, What makes a good story are dilemmas of human characters. Technology plugs in to our motives and motley emotions.

I congratulate Nidhi on publishing her second collection of crime fiction stories. Her dogged dedication to the craft of writing is commendable. I hope that it motivates her fellow writers to be more disciplined. And as her mentor, I am proud and happy to have played a small role in this journey.

Rashmi Bansal
October 2024

Preface

Thank you, dear reader, for making me an author.

Of all the things I thought I would be, 'Bestselling author' was too aspirational.

The success of the two books has been very humbling. Beyond words. Which is perhaps why one is so tongue-tied at the moment.

I hope you enjoy these stories.

I would LOVE to connect. I'm just an email away - authnidhi@gmail.com and on Insta, as **@authnidhi.**

That you have this book in your hand means that we are definitely like-minded.

Much Love,

Nidhi

August 2024

PS: Nothing in this book is in the realm of fantasy. Every behaviour of or using AI that you read in the book – has either already happened or can happen using the current technology.

Acknowledgements

First, of course, to God, who fulfilled a childhood dream of mine, albeit in a very different genre from the one I had in mind. I wanted to be published one day. The first poem was published when I was perhaps 15. But the books that have come out and have been appreciated, are in an altogether different genre - cyber security, AI, and crime.

Next, to **Rashmi Bansal**, my writing teacher.

The next is **Ishaan**, the child who patiently read all my stories and gave the go ahead. He commented on the plots, gave feedback on the language (Your plots are so cutting-edge, but your language is so ancient!), and ensured that I stayed the course.

T Sat, who patiently hand-held me through the journey, answering noob questions with patience.

My editor, **Jalpa Shah,** who defies description. I am SO lucky to have her in life – as an editor, and a friend.

CHAPTER ONE

The Will of Roshan Dalal

There are two ways to address a person. When he is a struggling businessman, he is Roshan Bhai[1]. When he becomes the owner of a mansion, a few luxury sedans, and a 500-crore company, he is Roshan Seth[2].

And that, ladies and gentlemen, was the life journey of Roshan Dalal – from Roshan Bhai to Roshan Seth.

Roshan was born to middle class teacher parents. His schooling and childhood were, therefore, driven by discipline and not cars.

In college, he showed the first signs of temporary insanity by declaring to his parents that he would do his CA but not join a stable job after that. That he would like to do a small trading business instead.

In India, there are distinct stereotypes that salaried and businesspeople hold about each other. As any salaried person would tell you, all businessmen are crooks and are not to be trusted. Roshan's parents also tried to tell him that.

But he was determined to be a businessman.

For five years after college, he tried to set up a profitable trading business. He profited a lot from the lessons learnt through his failures, but financial profit was not written in the destiny of Sumitra Trading Company (named after Roshan's mother, who else?!)

Then, he swallowed his pride and joined a rich merchant as an underling. He had a small job in the accounts department, but he made it a point to talk to the warehouse folks every chance he got. For a trading company, the warehouse is their place of business. Not the office. The office is for people who are not required for the running of the business.

After a few months, he requested Seth ji to give him additional work in the warehouse. He offered to file all incoming challans and outgoing gate passes on the spot without letting it affect his other work in any way. All he wanted was a cabin close to the gate, so he could get the papers as soon as something was going in or out.

The Seth was a kindly man who perhaps saw the spark in Roshan. Or, he was so disappointed in his own son that his soul was itching for a protégé. Either way, Roshan and the Seth developed a bond that was based on Roshan's industriousness and the Seth's mentoring.

That was the turning point of his life. From there, Roshan became Roshan Bhai, and before the age of 45, Roshan Seth.

The family had grown equally well. Roshan married – a good, arranged match. His family life was adequately happy.

The family was made up of Roshan, his wife Deval, their son – Deven (Deval + Roshan, of course), and their daughter – Reva, who was 5 years younger than Deven. The group was completed by Hemant – Roshan's nephew.

Hemant was perhaps Roshan's way of paying it forward. Roshan's sister had married a school teacher, as per the dowry ability of her parents. But her son, Hemant, had shown an aptitude for business. Seeing his interest and hard work, Roshan had offered to mentor him. Hemant completed his basic undergraduate degree and moved to Ahmedabad to learn from Roshan.

Deven, on the other hand, was a computer science engineer from ULB – one of the best universities in the US. He completed his studies and then joined his father's business as Head of IT, but also started an AI firm of his own – long before AI became a thing.

However, Ahmedabad is to AI what Maine is to startups. There simply is very little scope. So, after two years of frustration, Deven moved to Mumbai and then to Bengaluru. Reva was now married and led the marketing and sales unit of the holding company[3]. But she did not come home with Roshan Seth after work. Hemant did.

****

It was in these circumstances that Roshan Seth suffered a sudden heart attack on the 11th of February 2023.

The family was in shock. But after Covid, heart attacks had become so common, even among the youth. At least he went in peace. There was no suffering. He had dinner with the family as usual, cracked a few jokes, caught up with work, went to sleep, and just never woke up.

After the family had completed the 13th day ceremony, Deval gave gifts to all the family members[4] before they left. Hemant's mother asked him if he would like to come home now, but he politely told her that his life was with Roshan Mamu[5], and after him, with his family.

The next day, it was time to read the will and make new appointments, deal with the financial issues, and do the other things that needed to be done.

The will was read by Rustomji, the family solicitor of the Dalals. Rustomji Senior himself had passed just last year, and his son, Dorab Rustomji, was trying to take care of his father's practice and deal with his own grief. The death of Roshan uncle had also hit him hard.

"This will was made many years ago. But he never made a new will thereafter. So, this is the most recent will in our possession."

At this point, Dorab cleared his throat, "It is a formality for me to ask that if any of you has, or is aware of, a more recent copy of the will, please bring it in the open now, or this will remain the last known will and testament of Shri Roshan Dalal."

No one spoke.

Dorab opened the will and started reading it.

After customary gifts to long-serving staff, Roshan had made generous bequests to all his siblings and cousins, including Hemant's mother.

The businesses were to be divided in this way:

Roshan's share in the holding company which owned all group companies, was to be split into three parts and divided between Deval, Deven, and Reva.

The Managing Director's role, that Roshan held but Hemant executed, was to go to Deven, after training by Hemant.

Hemant was to get full control of a rayon fibre factory which was among the most profitable manufacturing businesses of the group. The holding company was to transfer all its stock in this rayon fibre company to Hemant. After the transfer, Hemant was to become 100% owner of the factory and all its assets.

The existing debt of that company, if any, was to be paid off by the holding company before transferring ownership.

In short, Hemant was to get a profitable, running company all to himself, debt free.

The rayon fibre factory was in a different part of Gujarat. Hemant would have to move there, while Deven would have to shut shop in Bengaluru and move to Ahmedabad. Both brothers were unhappy.

***

While preparations were being made to complete the paperwork, one morning, Dorab Rustomji made an urgent call to Deval. "Aunty, can you please come to my office immediately?"

"What is it, Dorab?"

"Just come, please."

Deval reached the office.

Dorab showed her a printout of an email. It was sent from Roshan's personal email ID to the official email ID of Dorab. No one was marked a copy.

The email read:

Dear Dorab

If you are reading this, I am probably gone.

Tomorrow, I hope to get a full test done, and also reach out to you for a new will. In the meantime, I am scheduling this email to reach you because this is important to me.

I want my assets to be divided in the following way:

A. In the holding company, all my shares go only to my wife, Deval, no one else.

B. Hemant will retain the Managing Director position for the holding company and retain his current role. The salary will be fixed by the Board, but it will not be below XXXXXXX.

C. In the subsidiary companies, the three children will get my shares in the following way:

.....

Followed by this text was a short list that divided the wealth, more or less, equally among Hemant, Reva, and Deven. But no one would need to move anywhere.

"But... how is this email coming now? So many days after he passed?" Deval asked in a shaky voice.

"Aunty, I think it was a scheduled email. Many people set up a scheduled email to reach their lawyer one month after the date of an angioplasty or open-heart surgery. This way, if they recover, they can always cancel the email. If they don't, it reaches us."

Dorab waited for the shock to subside. Then he spoke again.

"Aunty, this will is not legally admissible. To be legally valid, a will has to be signed physically, in the presence of two witnesses, who then need to attest the will. So, we can simply bury this email and no one will know. But I had to let you know. I could not take this decision myself."

Deval replied, "Thank you, Dorab. Let me think about this. If we do decide to honour his wishes, is that legally possible through the current will? "

"No, aunty. The inheritors will have to do that paperwork on their own. Deven and Reva will have to gift their shares to you, and so on. All individual transactions. We cannot make this will stick."

"Ok. I will think and come back to you."

For over two weeks, there was no communication. Dorab continued with the paperwork based on the physical will because that would anyway need to be completed, irrespective of Deval's decision.

***

In the meantime, Deval got her children together and shared the email printout with them.

"No, no, this can't be right. Dad never discussed this with us. He hadn't even booked a test for Saturday. There is something wrong with the email." Reva was the first to speak.

Deven nodded.

A forensic psychologist[6] was engaged. He went through the email and confirmed that this would be a 90% match to how Roshan Seth used to write his emails. No one could copy a style that much, even if they were living with them for many years.

Thereafter, a white hatter[7] went through the email trail and confirmed that:

A. The email was indeed scheduled on Friday night, near the bedtime of Roshan Seth.

B. The email was sent from the IP address[8] of the house.

C. The email was sent from a laptop, which was Roshan Seth's preferred device. He rarely wrote emails on his phone.

So, the authenticity of the email was confirmed.

The children were livid. This would make a significant difference to their wealth. Also, Dad's original will meant that Hemant would not play an active role in their lives any more. That was an astute thing to do, because the kids didn't get along as well as Hemant and Roshan Seth did. There was bound to be friction between the cousins, so it was best to reward Hemant with a profitable business all of his own, and leave the rest of the empire to the two children.

But Deval had a different view. "If this is what he wanted, then we should honour his wishes. I think we should do whatever he wanted in the email will."

Hemant was, understandably, kept out of the loop.

For more than a week, the kids and the parent went back and forth, neither agreeing to the entirety of the other's proposal.

Finally, they got Dorab involved. Dorab did not have the wisdom of his father, but he was, nonetheless, a sharp lawyer and a pragmatic man.

"I think there is a lot of middle ground where you all can meet. I fully agree that Reva and Deven will not be able to work with Hemant. That will lead to bitterness among cousins. It takes a long time and a lot of mutual dependence to create a working relationship. Aunty, please allow Hemant to move to his factory and run it fully.

That factory's debt is not too much. We can pay it off.

And to honour Uncle's wishes, we can always give Hemant some shares in the subsidiary companies. The holding company's shares can remain with you, Aunty, only you. Since you have got them from Uncle, under the law, they will necessarily pass only to your children on your death. So, it doesn't matter. My suggestion would be, don't give him anything in the holding company. That should be all yours, or it can remain with your children. Doesn't matter. The house is entirely yours anyway.

We can divide the subsidiary company shares in the way Uncle's will states. It's almost a three-way split between the 3 children."

"No. We will not give him one-third exactly if he is also getting the factory completely. Dorab, please give him some shares in a subsidiary company, and let the rest be divided among Deven and me. This way, he has the factory all to himself, debts paid and all, and he gets some shares also. I think that's fair." Reva interjected.

And so, it was agreed.

Suddenly, Deven asked, "Dorab, do you mind showing me the original email on your laptop? I would like to see it."

Dorab opened his laptop and showed them the email. He also forwarded it to the personal ids of all three of them.

"Just give me a week, Dorab, before you start the paperwork on the new arrangement."

"But we've already gone through forensics and investigations....." Dorab started to say.

"Yes, but I just realised something. A week. I promise." Deven interjected.

Dorab nodded and left.

***

A week later, Dorab and Deven were sitting in the lounge area of a suite booked for the meeting. Dorab was shaking his head in disbelief.

"Unbelievable! This has to be the most genius application of a new technology. The thing is, there is no law to govern this. Like, we can prove that the two outputs are very similar. But we cannot prove that Hemant did this, and that he was responsible for the email. My God, Deven! Legally, this is the perfect fraud. Psychologically, it is brilliant – to create something that is not legally valid but still creates doubt. And he successfully managed to fool me and your mom!"

Deven shared his findings with his mother and sister.

Deval was dumbfounded. She could not believe that the nephew who had been loved and cherished, had plotted like a mastermind.

"How would he have done this, Deven?" she asked.

"Ma, this is a solution that learns from you. Hemant had access to Dad's emails, because Dad marked him a copy on all his official emails. All he had to do was to spend a couple of hours every day training the algorithm in Dad's communication style. I haven't tried it myself, but a good guess would be, if I started today, within 8-10 weeks, I should be able to get this program to write a will exactly as you would like it. We can try it, if you want?"

"Nah re[9]! I will write my own will with my own two hands when the time is right."

"But Bhaiya.." Reva piped in, "How did you know that this is how he had done it? In the list of 'Ways to write a fake will' – this won't even come up in the top 10,000. How DID you think of this?"

"I just took a shot. Chatbot 3 was released just two months before Dad passed away. I was already a registered user. So, I just searched the query – 'Write a will the way Roshan Dalal would, with the following terms.. '

It took four attempts, but finally, Chatbot 3 produced an output that was very close to the email sent by Dad. This meant that someone had to have trained the algorithm already. Dad's email and his style of communication is not available as a public document that chat algorithms will learn from automatically. Dad was not a very public figure. This was a prepared plan, carefully executed."

"Dad passed away on Saturday, but this email had already been scheduled by then. How did he know Dad was going to die?" Reva asked.

"This is the sad part. The training of the chatbot had been going on for some time. He may even have joined as a beta user, or in November, after the launch of Chatbot 3. The email was scheduled Friday night, using the scheduler feature of the email client. I think he would just create a scheduled post and then delete it before it was sent. It was a very laborious way of going about it, but a very sure one. No one would suspect a thing if it was a scheduled email. It's a no-brainer that he had Dad's credentials."

"Wouldn't Dad know that there were scheduled emails in his outbox?"

"Unlikely. Do you ever go to the scheduled or deleted tabs of your inbox? Since we do not, as a matter of habit, schedule outgoing emails, we don't check these folders at all. It's just a matter of knowing your victim."

"But this is crazy!! Roshan was in very good health. No one expected him to pass away like this!" Deval butted in.

"Actually, mom, he was not. His recent blood report came on Wednesday. He told us all was well, but the markers for heart were not. Dr. Sharma told me during the 13th day ceremony."

"Why didn't he mention it to us?"

"Dad truly underestimated it. Dr. Sharma said Dad laughed when he called to tell him that the blood markers were not OK and he needed to come in for a full heart check-up. Dad really didn't think there was anything to worry about. But here's the thing – the blood results came by email. So, only one other person could have seen them."

"And they were bad enough to start preparing for his death?"

"No idea, mom. I think he didn't want to take a chance. In fact, I hate to say it, but it's likely that he was training the Chatbot to create a fake will that he would have got Dad to sign on. The email was just the intermediate backup."

Deval was speechless.

Dorab had a final thing to ask, "WHY were you so sure the email was fake?"

"Isn't it obvious? Dad laughed when Dr. Sharma told him all was not well. He was not going to schedule any tests.

Also, if Dad wanted to change his will, he would have told Mom first. Not you.

So, I knew the email was fake all through. But how did he create it?

An article about Chatbot mentioned that it could be used to mimic the writing style of great leaders. That's where I got the idea. Given a large enough sample, it could learn the writing style of anyone! And it did! The guy almost made it!

But, here's the thing - a chatbot can predict what someone is going to say, but it's still not advanced enough to know whether he is going to say it at all." There was a twinkle in Deven's eyes as he signed off.

[1] Bhai – brother, a general way to address a gentleman who is roughly of the same age as the speaker.

[2] Seth – literally means, a rich merchant. Honorific address for a rich person or a person with some social standing.

[3] A holding company is a company that holds most shares of other smaller companies in a large group. For example, Tata Sons is the holding company that holds most shares of other Tata Group companies. Some family businesses create a privately owned holding company and make individual companies as public limited companies.

[4] In India, it is customary to give a small gift as a token of the memory of the departed person. Usually, it is something from the estate of the person.

[5] Mamu – mother's brother

[6] A forensic psychologist is a professional who tries to understand the psychology of people involved in an incident.

[7] A white hatter is a person who uses his/her hacking skills to help law enforcement – to prevent hacking, not do it.

[8] IP – Internet Protocol. Every device connected to the internet has an IP address that is unique. This is the way to reach that specific device. Usually, devices in a network share similar IP address, where only the last digits are different.

[9] No, Thank you!

Malti Marg

Malti Marg – the quintessential quiet street where the quiet comes from being very tony. The 80-foot-wide road was as unassuming as one could imagine. It looked no different from any other road in this part of the city – lined on both sides with pavements and old trees. There were a few stores – hardly 4 or 5, which managed a turnover of a few crores each per year. The houses on both sides had verandas, greenery, and mostly old-style construction. The average size of plots varied from one to three acres. No one could walk easily from the main gate to the house.

There was no traffic. With such large houses, there was no office crowd to go and come back. The shops had an exclusive clientele which was not likely to need valet parking.

Right now, Malti Marg was being watched on a 100-inch screen by the top police brass of Delhi. The visuals on the screen were not of a quiet street. Malti Street had just been the subject of 3 bomb blasts. More than 100 people were feared dead. The blasts occurred at 6:00 PM on a Friday evening, when the Delhi crowd just needed all avenues to reach home (pun intended).

Thanks to CCTV footage, the three cars carrying the bombs had been identified. They were all Audis. The number plates were fake, as expected. The models were top end, making the cars appear perfectly at home as they remained parked on the side of the road, taking their rightful place among peers.

The blasts had been very carefully engineered – the first and third went off almost simultaneously, while the one in the center waited a few seconds for people to start panicking before tearing them to smithereens.

The buildings near the bombs were unrecognisable.

A bomb blast in the capital city, at peak office time, with more than 50 on-the-spot casualties, was not a small event. As soon as the police radio transmitted the news, the top brass got into their cars. Some did not even bother to change into uniform. They already knew where they had to reach – Emergency Response Room.

As per protocol, the room was in operation within 15 minutes of the blast.

Trained police teams were already monitoring ham radio and sat phone (satellite phone) communications. Another team was in place, monitoring mobile and web traffic of telecom service providers. The perpetrators would be sure to spread the good news among the right people. So far, they had drawn nought.

"Has anyone taken responsibility?" one voice piped up.

"No"

"What do we know so far?"

"At least fifty people expected dead on the spot. CCTV footage you can see, sir, and we are checking if we can track the sales of those Audi vehicles."

"Don't bother. You will find that they were all stolen. But, how was there so much traffic on the road? This road never has traffic! I have myself passed it at 6.00 PM on some evenings. No traffic at all!" the seniormost officer's shock was evident in his voice.

Another officer, whom we will call Mr. B, heard this and looked sharply at the speaker. He was right. The number of casualties in this location should have been between zero and five, even with three blasts. It was the number of people dead that had made this a Class 1 Emergency.

He took a deep breath and then said, in a low voice, "Let's call Amit."

"Amit, who?"

"He is an external cybercrime consultant who works with us sometimes. He is able to zoom out, see the big picture, and find angles that we tend to miss. He had the idea for that predictive algorithm for financial fraud[1]. I don't know how he will help in this, but a hunch – I think he will be able to help."

"You know as well as I do that the location of this room cannot be leaked to anyone. How will you get him in?"

"Blindfolded. Or I can set him up on a virtual call."

"Can't our cybercrime team take this up? They are well trained!"

"It's not the training sir, Amit's head works differently. He will be able to see something in this. He will of course work with the cyber team if there is something for him here."

"This is not a cybercrime. It's a good old-fashioned bomb blast. We need to activate the informer network."

"Mr. M, if the bomb blast has happened, the informer network has already failed. We can always have both. Why don't you call and activate the network? This falls under your area. We are now 30 minutes into the golden hour[2]. This CCTV footage has not thrown up any suspicious faces, which means the trigger was either automatic or remote. Ok, B, you can vouch for this guy?"

"Yes."

"Get him in."

While B was trying to reach Amit, C, another officer, called his PA and passed on some instructions. The rest of the room looked at him curiously.

"That golden hour comment made me realise – our mastermind, if he is in India, would be at the airport now, waiting to board a flight. In the next 5 minutes, due to runway repair, all international flights from Delhi's international terminal will have been suspended for a short period. Inconvenience caused will be deeply regretted. Passengers will be requested to await further instructions.

Airport managers have been informed to notify CISF as soon as any passenger tries to book a domestic flight from inside the airport."

"But won't he book online?"

"Only if he, or she, suspects. Much easier to walk to the airport counter and casually enquire about a domestic air ticket. It's a chance. We're taking it."

In spite of the pall of gloom, a small smile went around the room.

"ISBT[3] also will not allow any out of state buses to ply for the next two hours. Bus passengers are patient people. They will grumble and then spread out their bedsheets on the floor. Plainclothes personnel are on their way right now to scour and monitor. The foot soldiers of this crime are most likely to be at ISBT."

"That's a good plan. I am happy to see the team working together so well." The leader of group contributed the positive stroke[4].

"Nepal border has been alerted," another voice echoed through the room.

"OK. Good work. Do we have anything from the ham radio and sat phones chatter?"

"No, sir. Nothing yet. In fact, radio silence – literally and figuratively."

"Keep listening."

****

Amit came on the virtual call. He had seen the images on TV, and was visibly disturbed.

B addressed him directly, "Amit, let me come to the point. I take Malti Marg on some evenings. I never pass more than 2-3 cars on the entire stretch. Sir just asked the right question – how come there were so many cars there today? Can you think of anything?"

Amit's eyes lit up. "It's a no-brainer, sir. I think I know how. Has any of the victims been identified?"

"One minute." B got on a call and came back to Amit within sixty seconds. "Yes, we have some identifications. What do you need?"

"Their Wiggle ID and password, from their families, if possible. Even 2-3 will do. I know what has happened, but need to verify from 2-3 cases."

A stifled but distinct voice rang through the room, "Right. Your family member just died a gruesome death. By the way, can you share their Wiggle ID and password?"

Perhaps there was some silent snickering in the room, but it was ignored by most others. This was no time for jokes. Anything that could be tried, should be.

B continued, "Amit, you get the cyber team to do this verification. You are saying that their Wiggle maps led them to this road, that is how there was so much traffic there today at the time of the bomb blast. I am sure that will check out. What I want from you is to explain HOW Wiggle maps got these people there. Were they specifically targeted, or were they randomly sent there? And most importantly, HOW was Wiggle maps manipulated? Is there a clue we can find to the identity of the group from there? Can you work on that angle?"

"Yes sir."

"OK."

Amit got in touch with the cyber team and reached their control center to work with them. One team worked to get Wiggle IDs and passwords from the relatives and verify their Wiggle Maps routes to confirm that they were, in fact, following the Wiggle Maps app at the time of the blast, and the app had led them there.

Amit was sitting in another room, watching the confirmations pop up on an LCD display in the main control center. On another display, the CCTV footage from the blast was playing in ultra slow motion on a loop. Amit noticed that all the cars were high-end models. Not all of them were luxury vehicles, but reasonably rich. The distinct absence of taxis was very noticeable. Each of these cars had a predictable target inside. Taxis would mean random targets.

In a while, he got the CCTV team to his room and requested them to play the CCTV footage from this road for the last seven days. On the previous Friday, the number of cars passing that road from six to seven PM was ten. Eight of those cars were in the blast today.

Immediately, he checked if any of the Wiggle ids belonged to these car passengers. Yes, some did. He checked the Wiggle Maps history and found that these people had been sent there by the Wiggle maps app last Friday also.

He skipped the footage for the weekend and came to Monday. Twelve cars. At least four repeats with today's victims. Tuesday – six cars, one overlap. Wednesday – Two cars, no overlap. Thursday – twenty cars, eight overlaps.

Wednesday was control day[5]. Without manipulation, this stretch would have only two-three cars at that time.

The traffic was being manipulated at least since last Friday. The cars were not random. But on the day of the blast, the CCTV showed at least sixty cars bumper to bumper on this stretch. Which could only mean that the earlier days were test runs[6].

He now knew that Wiggle maps got these specific victims to this road by simply showing them an empty road to their destination.

He called the cybersec team and asked them to find details about the owners of whatever car numbers were visible in the CCTV footage. Especially those that were repeats. Maybe they were chosen at random, maybe not.

His time, however, needed to be devoted to finding out HOW Wiggle maps was compromised without detection for more than one week. Hopefully, that might lead to the identity of the hackers.

Another team got cracking on finding any similar cases around the world.

This was going to be a long and busy night, but no one was complaining.

Residents of Malti Marg had opened their homes, converting them to makeshift hospital beds while the limited supply of ambulances took turns ferrying the victims to hospitals in the vicinity. The blasts were strong enough to total most of the cars and many of the buildings in the vicinity. Survivors, if any, were exceptionally lucky, and grievously injured.

***

In other news, a secure police room had Taimur (not his real name) seated in a chair. He had made the mistake of asking for a domestic ticket from the international terminal when the runway was temporarily closed for repairs. But it was not his fault. No one told him this scenario could arise. He was simply trying to follow orders – get out of India ASAP[7]. This stupid runway repair meant at least 3-4 hours in Delhi itself, then the backlog of flights would have slowly started to take off – at least one whole night. The fastest way would be to fly to Mumbai and pick up an international flight from there. But these cursed officers had picked him up for questioning. No matter. His training did not cover runway being closed for repairs. But it had extensively covered being picked up by Indian police.

He started breathing heavily with practised ease. His pulse raced. He asked for a hospital. Instead of being taken to a doctor, he was left locked in the room and the light of the room was switched off. But he wasn't scared at all. It might be his first mission for God, but his dedication was second to none.

One hour later, he was even more sure. He was just a young student, studying computer science. He had a long life ahead. Surely, God would want him to live, if for nothing else, then to continue the mission using his unique skills. This would all pass very soon. All he had to do was to keep quiet, repeat that he was completely innocent, and that he was being targeted because of his demographic. Very soon, #FreeTaimur would start trending on the microblogging site - Y.com, and the authorities would have no choice but to let him go.

***

In the Emergency Response Room, there was growing frustration.

ISBT produced no leads. Some young men had tried to leave quietly. It was found that they needed to reach Kanpur for their sister's wedding.

Ham radio and sat phones were both reporting only the normal chatter.

The darkweb[8] team crawling the regular forums was also, surprisingly, drawing very poor results. All the forums were abuzz with news of the strong blasts in Delhi, but no one seemed to be taking responsibility. There were the regular hate messages, but no one was bragging or thanking God yet. It was not just a long vigil. It was turning out to be a rather fruitless one.

****

Taimur's laptop was sent to Amit. He started forensics. This activity would tell him everything that the laptop had been used for.

He knew exactly what he was looking for on that image[9].

Thirty minutes later, he'd found it. He passed the information to Mr. B. The Response Team, predictably, had a skilled interrogator. The conversation with Taimur was about to begin even as the families of the killed were running from hospital to hospital, hoping against hope that their loved ones were among the seriously injured, not among the body parts.

***

In his room, Taimur was getting restless. The interrogator entered with some other senior officers in tow.

"Listen, child, we are not going to ask you what you did. We are going to tell you. Your parents, as you can see, are in that room. You folks can see each other. Feel free to communicate via signs and eyes.

You are a local Delhi boy – grew up here, know the city like the back of your hand. So, it was easy for you to tell the handler which street you wanted to target. He only had to make sure you had everything you needed to work peacefully, and maybe do a little legwork on your behalf.

You are not just a computer engineer in the making. You are, what is called a prompt engineer. Your job is to get AI to do your work by giving it the right prompt.

You did two things. First, you got Wiggle's own AI, Apollo, to write you the code to divert cars to a specific spot. I am not sure yet, but some of the features of these users were – they followed Wiggle maps regularly, they drove their own cars, most of these cars were high end, and their route was within four kilometers of this particular road.

With that, you had the first version of your code ready. Then, you created an add on that allowed you to run this code recursively – for multiple days at one go, with a separate target number for each day. When the target number of diversions was met, the program would stop working.

Recursive code was pure genius because this meant you only needed to inject once. No need to inject for each test run. Monitoring would be as simple as standing there, visiting one of the stores, or just hacking into one of the CCTV cameras on the road.

But you still had a problem. How to get into the cloud center[10] that hosts Wiggle maps and insert this code? The architecture of this solution is known only to a few company insiders.

And once again, you used prompt engineering. Using Wiggle's Apollo, you asked to write a code that would bypass the security architecture and allow an injected code to be added directly to the app's servers closest to India[11].

After that, you just had to run it.

I am sure you would have looked at your handiwork with a lot of satisfaction and pride. It was pure genius to ask a company's own AI to access internal documents and write out the injection code.

We know your identity and that of the handlers. We know where you were trained, and we have access to your WhatsApp chats.

You are a very intelligent young Indian. I think, child, that you need to make a decision."

Taimur laughed. He was going to be rescued. This was a joke.

****

A few weeks later, Mr. B was treating Amit to tea at the prestigious Delhi Club.

"Sir, one thing I am still trying to understand. They could have done this blast in Chandni Chowk or any other crowded market of Delhi. Where was the need to divert traffic to a quiet road and then do a bomb blast?" Amit was still wondering.

"Remember Mumbai, 26 November 2008?"

Amit nodded silently. The memory of those brethren dead was still too painful.

"Why Taj Palace Hotel and not Dadar or Matunga? For exactly the same reason, Malti Marg and not Chandni Chowk." Mr. B paused for a while before continuing, "Amit, in that moment of crisis, I somehow just knew you were the man for the job. I am saying the words, but the gratitude is from the entire team. Thank you, again![12]"

"Sir, actually, in this case, I did not crack the case. I did exactly what you asked me to do – Who was sent to their deaths, and How. You all cracked the case. All my information did not lead to the source. The source was from the officer who set up the airport trap. Had we not caught that boy, we would have been clueless."

"Amit, let me flip that scenario for you. We have the boy, but nothing to hold him on. It would have taken us hours to go through his hard drive and find his modus operandi. By then, the media would have screamed human rights, some group would have got him midnight bail, and we would have lost. We were able to close him because you figured out what you needed to look for on his laptop. We filed his paperwork within the hour. He is in jail now, awaiting trial.

So, it is like two pieces of a jigsaw – both are useless without each other. Please, take the credit, and another chai."

Amit dipped his head slightly to the side, "Thank you, sir!"

[1] The story – "The Diary of Amit Sharma – II" in this collection.

[2] The golden hour is the time right after an event, when the chance to salvage the situation is the highest. It is used for kidnappings, bomb blasts, heart attacks, strokes, and other time-sensitive events.

[3] Inter State Bus Terminal – the largest bus terminal in Delhi, where most inter-state buses reach and leave from.

[4] A positive stroke is the term used in Transaction Analysis to indicate a positive interaction between two people.

[5] In any experiment, when we do not influence any aspect, that is called the control group. In this case, Wiggle Maps did not send any traffic to the road on Wednesday. This means we get to see the regular, expected level of traffic on Wednesday.

[6] A test run is when we execute a program to test if it is working or not.

[7] As Soon As Possible

[8] Darkweb is the part of internet that is not indexed. It is usually used for illegal chats, crime, ransomware, selling stolen data, and other such activities.

[9] The copy of the hard drive of the compromised computer is called an image.

[10] The data center that stores this program and runs it.

[11] This is called prompt injection - https://arstechnica.com/information-technology/2023/02/ai-powered-bing-chat-spills-its-secrets-via-prompt-injection-attack/

[12] Amit Sharma has appeared in The Diary of Amit Sharma – II and in 'Probe8', in a story called the Diary of Amit Sharma.

CHAPTER THREE

Maja Ni Life

December 2023

Mr. Sampath was dead.

That should have been the last line of a screenplay of a 1970s Hindi film. But it was the start of this case.

The death of a widower living alone in one of the old bungalows of Hyderabad would usually not be of interest to the police. But Mr. Sampath had made his exit in a way that necessitated the entry of the police.

Mr. Sampath belonged to one of the older families of the city. His house – *God's Villa*, represented old Hyderabad grandeur – for good reason. It was built in 1921 by an ancestor (the great grandfather, to be precise).

The majestic white building was magically always pristine white. The well-kept garden was not as well-kept anymore, and the furniture was often found dusty – not for want of wages, but for want of attention. There is only so much an elderly person can check.

The call had been made by Jeetu ji, the long-time caretaker of Mr. Sampath. Jeetu ji was perhaps just a couple of years younger than Mr. Sampath. His father was the caretaker of the bungalow before him, and it was simply assumed that he would fill his father's shoes when the time came. He took his training from a young age, but always as a caretaker, not as a servant or anything. A caretaker is the most senior staff member in the household.

Jeetu ji had a small retinue reporting to him, though nothing like his father's times. But that was not needed now. Mr. Sampath's children lived in the US, and seldom visited. But Mr. Sampath visited them for 2-3 months in summer, so the family remained close. Since the death of his wife, Mr. Sampath had entertained only his bachelor friends once in a while, and who needs a full staff for that? With time, even that had reduced, as the friends, well, kicked the bucket - one after another. No shame in admitting the truth, no? Old folks die, and Mr. Sampath's friends were old, just like him.

Jeetu ji had found him in the courtyard. There was blood, so he knew that the first call would have to be made to the police. Then, he called Mr. Sampath's children in the US.

***

Inspector Reddy was a man of habit. Too much habit. Rumour was that his sensors were capable of measuring a difference of micrograms in the sugar added to his morning tea. While this made life difficult for people working with him, it made his own life very easy. Habit creates predictability and predictability takes away stress.

At *God's Villa*, the first thing that hit Reddy was how much cooler it was as soon as they entered the gate. 'Planting trees does work,' he thought to himself.

The driveway led to the patio and the garages were just to the left. There were two garages. One of them held an old Toyota Camry, while the other held a modern Tex Model Y. Reddy was surprised to see the Tex Model Y. The car was not being sold in India yet. All models were imported. Only the very rich could afford this electric supercar. But

Mr. Sampath did not appear to be a driving enthusiast. For the moment, however, he said nothing.

Mr. Sampath was lying, slightly curled up and face down, about 20 feet from the garages – in the patio. The main injury, presumably, was at the back of the head. Not a pretty sight.

The patio was just a small brick and ivy cover over the driveway, right in front of the house, where one could board or alight from a car. An umbrella stand and a wooden stool on the side completed the patio scene.

After the forensics team had done its work, the ambulance took the body to the morgue. Jeetu ji, who had managed everything so far with equanimity, broke down when they started to lift Mr. Sampath. The police personnel helped him, consoled him, and offered him water.

And then began the investigation.

When Jeetu ji was in a slightly better state of mind, Reddy came to talk to him.

"I'm sorry Jeetu ji. This is a traumatic day for you."

Jeetu ji just nodded.

"Don't force yourself to think in any specifics. Tell me everything about him – anything that comes to your mind."

Jeetu ji took Reddy at face value. He started with the childhood of Sampath – as an only child. Studious, intelligent, diligent. He had done well academically and professionally. The family business was land-owning. They held huge tracts of land that were sub-let to farmers to cultivate. The rent was in part cash and part produce, so *God's Villa* was never short of food – staples and exotics.

Unlike other land-owners, the family took care of its tenant farmers. Did not penalize them for a bad crop. That's why they enjoyed higher rentals than others. People were more than happy to pay a little more just to be associated with the family. Even though the family only visited the village two or three times a year – on important festivals, no one dared to occupy their land illegally. In short, no enemies.

Sampath's children – a boy and a girl, were both educated and now lived in the US. They didn't want the land or the house. They were never coming back. So, now, Sampath had sold off parcels of land over periods of time and put the money in banks, from where a steady interest kept him provided for. There was no more land.

The house staff was minimal – Jeetu ji, one guard, one cook, and one cleaning person. Jeetu ji and the guard were the only full timers. There was also a driver who came on need basis. He was the son of a former servant. Sampath had saved him from going wayward by offering him a job and keeping him on the grounds. Within six months, the boy had straightened out and was able to find a better, higher paying job – with the commitment that on the day Mr. Sampath needed him, he would be there.

But Mr. Sampath only needed him when his kids came visiting – which was never. So, for the last couple of years, the driver had remained on call but had only been called to drop and pick up Mr. Sampath from the airport.

"What do his children do in the US?" Reddy asked.

"I have no idea sir. But I have called them up. They are on their way."

Reddy nodded, then pointed to the house, "Is anything missing, Jeetu ji? Any theft? The house is undisturbed, but you can identify if anything is gone. Would you like to take a look?"

"I did, sir. When your people were taking pictures and all, I did that only – went right around the house. Also checked the safe. No problem. Everything is in its own place. No theft as far as I can make out."

"How do you think the person entered?"

"We live in an old colony, sir. No one even locks their houses around here. The guard is supposed to sit at the gate but is more often found playing cards with the other guards and drivers of the colony. There is no crime to be prevented here. The gate is usually open. These days, Srinu, our guard, is away on his annual leave. But it didn't make any difference to us. The main gate is an iron thing. I just turn the bolt from the outside if I go out anywhere, which is rare. The driveway, as you can see, leads to the house. The door of the house is made of wood. It has two bolts – one electronic and one mechanical, but usually none of them are fastened. We have no CCTV or anything."

Inspector Reddy sighed.

"One more thing, Jeetu ji. That car – the Tex Model Y, is the latest thing. It is imported, but Mr. Sampath does not sound like a driving enthusiast...."

"That was Raju baba's gift to his old man. Just last month, it arrived. Sampath sir was muttering all the time about wastage of money and all that, but Raju baba would have none of it. Our Camry is old and reliable, but this new car is automatic with a lot of features that make driving easy for old people. And no need to go to petrol pump also. The charging point is right here – in the house."

"Very nice! So, did Mr. Sampath take the car out for a spin?"

"Oh, yes! The day it came, we charged it full and then all of us in the house went for a drive – Sampath sir, me, and Srinu.

Then, two days later, Sampath sir took it out for a drive alone, and came back very happy.

Then, one week later, he took some friends out. After ages the oldies got out together and they all looked so happy. So, yes, he was using it."

"When did Srinu leave for his break?"

"Ten days ago, I think, sir. I will check. We don't really pay attention to dates anymore."

"Ok. Can you think of ANY reason that one would want to hurt Mr. Sampath?"

Jeetu ji shook his head in the negative.

"So, to sum up, no enemies, no security, no CCTV cameras – anyone could have walked in, done this, gone out, completely unnoticed?"

Jeetu ji shook his head in the affirmative.

Reddy let out another sigh.

"I'm sorry Jeetu ji, this is my toughest question for today – where were you last night?"

"I have a room on the other side – behind the house. It has a small kitchen and an attached bathroom. Sampath sir does not like anyone in the main house at night. So, yesterday, I served him dinner as usual – at about eight o'clock or so, then cleared up, and I think it must have been about nine when I locked the iron gate and went home. Sampath sir was in the hall, reading a book. I never saw him alive again."

"And that padlock was untouched this morning?"

"Yes, the padlock was untouched this morning. But it's just a 4-feet-high gate, sir. Anyone could have jumped over it."

"How and when did you find him? Run me through step by step."

"Morning, about seven or so, I walked from my room to the iron gate as usual. The milk and newspaper are left in a bag that we leave hanging on the main iron gate. I picked them up, unlocked the gate, and walked towards the house. This is what I do every day. Sampath sir is sometimes sleeping, sometimes in the garden, sometimes in a chair in the hall, with the window open. His sleep has been very unpredictable the last few years. I saw him as I neared the house... and there he was... the blood told me immediately that there was no point in looking for a pulse or anything. I saw the wound later. The blood.... "

At this point, Jeetu ji paused. Reddy gave him time.

After a while, he resumed, "Then, I called the police from my mobile phone. After that, I called his children. Then, I sat down here..." he pointed to a place on the side of the driveway. Presumably, this is where the body would have come into view.

"You did not go into the house or anything?"

"Sahab[1], making those three calls was more bravery than I thought was possible for me. It is a great achievement that I am not dead of a heart attack too... all that blood..."

"One small thing.. his face was down.. how did you know it was Mr. Sampath and not someone else?"

Jeetu ji looked at Inspector Reddy as if he was insane, "Who else would it be? Actually, I didn't think that much. I saw him, knew it was him, and called. That was all the wits I had about."

"Do you drink, Jeetu ji?"

"Every Friday night. With my buddies. Not in the house. Sampath sir does not like drinking."

With that, the interview ended.

***

The more Reddy heard, the less he liked the case. One random old person who lived alone, troubled no one, dead with a single blow to the back of the head. No theft, nothing.

The interviews with the other staff members and neighbours had also been inconclusive. No enemies. No grudges. No threats. Very little social life. Stayed home most days. Read a lot. Had regular and simple food habits. Not too many valuables in the house.

Inspector Reddy knew that in such colonies, neighbours very rarely met socially. So, he was not surprised. But it was one more dead end, and he did not like dead ends.

There were motley beggars and ragpickers who frequented the colony. None of them had seen anything suspicious. The colony guards and drivers had not observed anything different. They had not seen anyone jump the gate (to be fair, they wouldn't know. Most guards slept at night.)

The postmortem was conclusive – death around midnight, single blow to the back of the head, no other struggle marks. He probably collapsed immediately. No murder weapon found, but likely to be a lathi[2] or something similar.

The children came and saw their father with so much pain in their eyes that Inspector Reddy found it hard to face them.

The final rites were performed. After the forty-day mourning period was over, the children handed over the keys to Jeetu ji and requested him to find buyers for the property. Then they flew out. They did not meet the police or even request them to find the murderer. Somehow, Reddy found that more insulting than if they had pressurised him.

***

February 2024

Reddy HATED cold cases like this. Not ONE lead. Not one clue. Just.. nothing.

After two months, the case file was closed ... inconclusively.

***

February 2024

"Maja ni life![3]" Abhishek muttered contentedly as he stretched his arms to their full width, taking in the beautiful garden outside his window. Since taking this gig, he had been able to pay attention to the garden.

His job was simple, really. He worked at a third-party tech company. The client was a high-tech car company working towards self-driving cars. How does one make a self-driving car work? One trains the sensors of the car to correctly identify objects in the vicinity. Then, one teaches the engine the correct responses to those objects or stimuli. Abhishek's job involved the former – object identification.

Because it was confidential, he was not allowed to sit in an office where others might see his feed. He had to work from home.

There were two types of tasks – the first involved watching the videos and tagging the objects and movements correctly. The second involved checking the tagging done by the AI engines of the cars and indicating whether the identification was right or wrong.

On an average day, he identified and/or corrected about 100-150 items.

To say that this job was a full-on entertainment show would be an understatement. Unlike other cars, the cams on this beauty were motion, sound, and light activated. Which meant that they turned themselves on as soon as any one of these things happened, and recorded video. The clips were recorded "for training and research" even if the cars themselves were switched off (Oh, the beauty of a battery!)

These video clips were sent to the research/observation team. Sometimes, the cars took only pictures. Abhishek didn't know why it was pictures sometimes and video most other times, but he didn't care either.

But there was a HUGE backlog. Like, they were still processing videos from November – December 2023. Some days, he liked to randomly pick up more recent videos. But that was only for variety. He knew he needed to close the task list of the day before the end of the 8-hour work shift. So, he usually stuck to the roster.

Each video was sent to two to five human observers. Their selection and assignment were completely random, except that at least one had to belong to the geography of the recording and one could NOT be from the geography of the recording.

The folks were not allowed to talk to each other officially, nor share digital media with each other. But when had that stopped IT folks? The research employees had made a Discord[4] server on which screen grabs and videos were freely shared.

What was shared on these Discord servers was pure gold – people in their underwear, couples arguing, couples making out, kids on bonnets... Oh! People had no idea their cars were recording even when they were switched off, and what fun they all had! (To be fair, people also had no idea that 'research and training' meant random hoomans[5] looking at their videos and 'tagging' stuff like 'underwear', 'angry', etc.)

But this Monday, even Abhishek thought that Dan888 had crossed all limits. He was so smitten by the young lady in the video that he had noted down the geotagging of the video, then used Google maps to accurately pinpoint her house. Thankfully, she lived over the Atlantic Ocean – a distance that Dan888 could not cover - given his limited means. Abhishek had been disgusted when Dan888 shared the Roadview[6] image of the house. He had considered whistle blowing[7], but then decided he wasn't a snitch. He just sent a message to OG, the informal group leader, asking him to rein in Dan. There was honour even among thieves.

***

On Friday, however, Abhishek was in a completely different frame of mind. He had just seen a video for the third time. And he was frozen. Completely FROZEN.

He was sure he had identified what he was seeing accurately – even in the night vision camera view.

The scene was simple and the duration was short. A scruffy looking man entered the frame from the right. Scruffy man exited frame into the darkness. An old man entered frame from the left. Old man looked around. He looked confused. Suddenly, scruffy man reappeared behind the old man and hit the old man on the head with what appeared to be a largish stone. Old man dropped to the ground almost immediately. Scruffy man looked around and quickly made exit towards the right, where he had entered from. That was it. That was the whole video. If a subsequent video had been recorded, it was not in his task list.

Was the old man safe? Who was he? Where did this happen?

Too many questions. Should he report the video? What will the company do?

With trembling hands, he called his supervisor.

"Yes, Abhishek.. tell me?" his manager was usually to the point.

"Sir, I have just seen a video. I think you should see it too. It is important. I think it is a murder being recorded."

The line was silent for just a few seconds before the response came, "Abhishek, you know I cannot see your video on account of strict confidentiality clauses we have with the client. Further, it would be unethical. Please process the video as per our SOP[8]s."

"But, sir, we need to make sure that the old man is ok. He was attacked!"

"Abhishek, when is the video from?"

Abhishek noted the date with dismay, "December, sir."

"Then, either way, we cannot help the old man, can we?"

"Yes, sir." Abhishek muttered and hung up.

He processed the video as per SOP. "Bludgeon", "Grievous hurt" – none of these verbs were in the word list. There was just one word that appeared relevant – 'Violence'. He marked that and moved on.

***

But he could not sleep. Not that night. Nor the night after. Not that he considered himself a sensitive man, but he needed closure. Was the old man safe? Was he saved? What happened to him?

Finally, in a flash, he realised what he could do. He searched the meta data of the video, found the geotag, and using Roadview, found the house that the geotag referred to. To his surprise, he found that the property was large, so there was no chance of mistaking the house where the crime took place. "I think he was ok. No way one lived alone in such a large house. Am sure someone from the house saw him." Abhishek smiled to himself.

Just to be sure, he hit news search and zeroed in on the city and date of the video, with a week before and after, using the relevant keywords – senior citizen, attacker, etc.

But the reports that came up were assorted. He was surprised to see how many old people were attacked in a city in a day. Only the successful assaults made it to the news. None of the unsuccessful attacks made it to the news. "This is good! If I don't find the right piece of news, it means that the old man must have been saved!"

But that was not how it ended, of course. He added the name of the house to his search, and voila! The news items of Mr. Sampath's death came right up. The old man hadn't made it. Worse still, the news mentioned that the unknown attacker had never been found.

NOW Abhishek was in the middle of a moral dilemma. He realised that he was the only one who could solve the murder case of Mr. Sampath. But, doing that would mean losing his job and worse still, his company losing the contract with Tex. That would mean hundreds of jobs gone. Was it worth it? One unsolved murder from months ago?

***

Abhishek took a screen recording of the video anyway. Ironically, the person he reached out to was Dan888, not OG.

On the video call, Dan888 was a very normal looking young man. He heard Abhishek out and was silent for a while. Finally, he spoke, "Dude, what do you want to do?"

"I want to share this video with the police. It might help them."

"You know that Tex will never approve this. We cannot let customers know we are filming them even when the cars are off, to train our AI model."

"I know that, Dan. But this could help solve a murder!"

"You think so? How?"

"Well, they have the guy in the frame! We know what he looks like!"

"So? We know what he looks like. We don't know who he is." Dan was deadpan.

"I am sure the police will know who he is."

"Why are you so sure? Does your country have national facial recognition software like China?"

"Hell, No!"

"Exactly. Forget all this and focus on your work. This is pointless."

Abhishek thanked Dan for his time and ended the call.

Perhaps to give closure to himself, Abhishek created an anonymized email ID, uploaded the video to that email ID, and kept it in drafts[9].

And that was how, for the second time, the case file on the Sampath Murder case was closed.

***

March 2023

There can be many theories to explain what happened next. Miracle, destiny, Mr. Sampath's soul coming back for justice, coincidence – you, dear reader, may take your pick. We will stick to telling you what happened.

Abhishek's company had an offsite. The location of the offsite was a resort in Hyderabad.

The company was rewarding all researchers for a year of great performance.

The offsite was due to start on Friday, but the travel desk made a mistake and booked Abhishek on the Thursday morning flight. This meant that he had one extra day compared to his colleagues. His manager, in a rare display of generosity, told him to stay the extra day at the property and have fun.

From that point on, everything conspired to take Abhishek to Inspector Reddy. Part effort, part destiny.

Abhishek started by taking a taxi to the location that he had seen on Roadview. He recognised the house immediately, but was stunned by the change in the grounds.

Roadview showed the grounds as being decently maintained – lots of trees and well-kept shrubs. But this was an overgrown jungle. No maintenance at all.

The main gate was locked from the outside. It was a small iron gate, nothing special. He started to look around, but Hyderabad in March is not the time for folks to be outdoors. The street had large houses, and it was obvious that the residents, guards, and visitors – everyone believed in afternoon siestas that started at 10:00 AM and ended only after 4:30 PM.

The nearest shop for water was at least 500 meters away and his taxi was already gone.

The only way to not get a heatstroke would be to order another taxi and go around the location, trying to figure something out. He put his hand in his pocket and froze. His wallet was missing. He had taken it out, paid the taxi guy, then a call had come – some stupid tele-caller, and he had alighted while shouting at the tele-caller. So, the wallet was probably still in the taxi.

The first step, of course, would be an FIR[10] for the identity documents. He called another radio taxi and made his way to the nearest police station.

Usually, Inspector Reddy would be out on one of his cases. But on this day, he had suffered a nosebleed in the morning and was forced to stay inside the police station.

After Abhishek had filed his FIR, he looked around and suddenly realised that he had hit the jackpot. He was in the police station that had jurisdiction over the house!

God knows what got into him, but he asked the police person directly, "There was a death in a house called *God's Villa* some months ago. Was the case solved?"

While the Havildar recording his FIR looked up at him archly, Inspector Reddy, who had overheard this statement, reacted completely differently. He put a strong arm on the shoulder of the young man and beckoned him to follow. The young man was brought ceremoniously to the cabin of the inspector himself – a matter of great honour. Then, he was offered chai – another great honour.

Then, he was asked how he knew about the case and what his interest was.

It was in that moment that Abhishek realised what an epic bad situation he had put himself into. Was he sure he wanted to share the video with the police? And, was it possible to turn back from here? The answer to both questions, unfortunately, was, 'No'.

Fortunately for him, Inspector Reddy was a good reader of people and a very observant person. From the shadow that flashed across the young man's face, he knew this was a case of someone knowing something, but not sure of sharing it with the police.

He worked his practiced magic, and within fifteen minutes, Abhishek was showing him the video of the assault, having confessed that an entire company could possibly shut down if the video leaked.

Inspector Reddy could not believe his eyes. He knew this guy. He was one of the regular ragpickers of the colony. He had questioned this guy after the attack!

There was no need for him to even use the video! He could make the guy crack with just the threat of an eyewitness who has come forward now. That was it!

Abhishek and Inspector Reddy shook hands and exchanged numbers.

The rest, as they say, is history. The genius rag picker was still in the same lane. When confronted with the possibility of an eyewitness, he cracked.

It wasn't much of a confession, but for what it's worth, here's a gist:

He didn't have money for drugs, so he thought he'd try his luck. *God's Villa* had only two people living. Srinu was out. It was worth a shot. He jumped over the gate, made his way to the main door, and then started looking for something small, near a window, that he could just pick up and jump out again, just for a small fix.

But at that moment, the old man came out and started looking for him. In that drug-starved state, he just picked up a nearby stone, sneaked up to the old man, and hit him on the head. The man went down without so much as a whimper.

But once it was done, he realised, even in that stupor, that he had done something terribly wrong. He ran to the main gate, jumped out as quickly as possible, ran to the nearby pond, dropped the stone, came back to his place in the street, and slept. If anyone noticed he was gone, they assumed he'd gone to look for a dealer and come back. No one would associate violent murder with a rag picking druggie.

The next morning, he just had to pretend to be as stunned as everyone else. That was all. There was no question of running away, because that would have alerted the police to possible guilt. He had remained, doing his rag picking and street sleeping as usual.

***

Inspector Reddy filed the papers, shaking his head. His team could never figure out if the shaking of the head was for the wrong dosage of sugar in his tea, or the pointlessness of yet another stupid violent crime.

[1] Sir

[2] A type of stick used in combat.

[3] This is the good life!

[4] Discord is an app that allows people to chat in text, talk in audio-video, and share content with each other. It is popular among the youth.

[5] An informal spelling for humans. Used by dog lovers and some modern social media users.

[6] An application that maps roads and civil areas all over the world and gives a realistic view of how the place looks to a visitor – using real images and videos. Roadview is a fictitious name. The service exists under another name.

[7] When someone is doing something that is wrong, calling it out is called whistle blowing. Typical whistle blowing includes talking about corruption in a company, showing malpractices of a company, etc. A whistle blower is typically an insider – an employee.

[8] Standard Operating Procedures – the prescribed way to do any work.

[9] When an item is kept in drafts, its contents are not flagged even if someone is monitoring network traffic.

[10] First Information Report – Police report

CHAPTER FOUR

The Kidnapping Story

"Hello!"

"Listen, Shravya's not come home yet. Her phone is also coming switched off[1]."

"And you disturbed me in office to tell me this? Unbelievable! Bharati, she's a teen now. She must be hanging out with friends and her phone must have run out of battery. Chill. It's not even 3:00 PM! She'll come home. Don't worry about it." Vinay cut the call.

If paranoia had a name, Bharati would be it. Always paranoid. 'Don't put music videos on that musical app, don't put YouTube videos of dance covers, don't go out late at night, don't do this, don't do that..' Sheesh!

He switched to WhatsApp to distract his mind from the irritation for two minutes. Might as well check some messages and change the mood also. There was one from an unknown number. "Another sales spam!" he muttered to himself while opening it, but the thumbnail on the video was his daughter, Shravya. So, he clicked on the video.

It was Shravya all right. She was seated in a chair. Her hands and feet were tied with strips that appeared to be canvas – thick and hard. Shravya had a plaintive look on her face and looked very, very scared. She was staring into the camera, but for the first ten seconds, said nothing. Then, very slowly, she said, "Papa, please give these guys what they want. I don't know where I am, but they are saying it's a financial transaction only. They will let me go once you pay them. Please, please pay them."

His feet rooted to the spot, Vinay simply froze. With shaking hands, he tried Shravya's number. It was switched off. He pulled out his alternate phone from the pocket and tried her number again. Still switched off. He went back to the message and played the video again. And again. He was panicking AND trying to find clues at the same time. The location was really dark. He could not make out any other furniture in the setting, nor could he figure out the source of light on Shravya's face. Was it natural? LEDs? Where was it coming from? He couldn't make out a thing! What a stupid, stupid father he was!

There was another message on the chat: "Five bitcoins. By 5:00 PM."

One minute later, another message: "At 5:30 PM, it will be 53 bitcoins. After that, it will be too late."

He tried calling the number using the WhatsApp call feature. Obviously, the call was rejected. His daughter's kidnappers were not willing to talk to him. He had no idea how many there were, how old, or even if they were men or women.

He tried the number from an office landline. No response.

That was the moment reality sunk in. His daughter was out there somewhere, and he had two hours to arrange five bitcoins.

Immediately, he responded to the WhatsApp chat – "Arranging Money. In the meantime, please take good care of her."

***

Vinay pulled out his laptop and did a quick calculation. At today's price of 28,000 USD per bitcoin, he was looking at 1.12 crore rupees. He had two hours to arrange 1.12 crores, convert them to Bitcoin, and transfer them to a specific wallet.

He called up Bharati, "Listen, Bharati, Shravya is with some people. But don't worry. All they want is money, and I am arranging it. Don't panic, please. Let me deal with this. I will bring her home safe and sound. Promise." Bharati disconnected without saying a word.

***

The next call was to his investment advisor, Sachin – "How much money do we have in crypto now?"

Sachin was surprised. This was very unlike Vinay. However, to Vinay, he said, "One minute. Let me check. You are at ... 2 bitcoins now."

"OK, how soon can you convert some of my assets to 3 more bitcoins and transfer them to a wallet on Coinvase[2]?"

"Vinay.. are you under a ransomware attack?" Sachin didn't take long to understand.

"Just tell me the time it will take please."

"OK, give me five minutes, I will come back to you. But I do urge you to get the police involved. Ransomware gangs usually do not return the data even after paying the ransom. Five bitcoins is too little. Call you back asap. Take care."

The third call was to his friend. "Aryan, I need a favour – urgently. It's about my daughter.."

Aryan dropped whatever he was doing and put his phone on speaker.

***

Vinay was the success that business magazines rarely talked about. Good education pedigree supplemented by a successful family business that he had taken over. The business had grown. Not exploded or reached stellar heights, but grown. In time, he married his childhood sweetheart, Bharati, and they now had two children – Yash, 7, and Shravya, 16.

Aryan was his childhood friend. Vinay knew that Aryan knew some people in the police. Hence, the call.

***

Sachin called Vinay back in fifteen minutes instead of five, but with good news. They could convert to cash within the next thirty minutes. Vinay gave the go-ahead and instructed Sachin to call him when he was ready to make the transfer to the wallet.

****

Aryan had, in the meantime, reached out to a police officer in the police station that had jurisdiction over Vinay's area, and discussed the case with him. When Vinay reached the police station ten minutes later to file an FIR, he found someone waiting for him. Bharati had also reached. They held hands for just a brief moment, each lending their strength to the other.

Within ten minutes, the FIR was filed, and Vinay's phone was sent to the forensics team to try and trace the WhatsApp number that had sent the video. The video itself was sent for forensic analysis to see if it contained any meta-data that indicated the location, time of making the video, type of camera used to make the video, etc.[3].

Surprisingly, the team came out blank. The video had no meta data at all! The kidnappers were smart.

A physical team was sent to the school. The school guard saw her photograph and confirmed that she was a student, and he did vaguely remember seeing her that day, but couldn't be sure if she was alone or with someone.

The last cell signal from her phone was barely 500 meters outside her school. But this area had some five-six side alleys, where there was hardly any movement. She could have been lured into any one of these.

The class teacher mentioned that Shravya was friendly with everyone in the class. She didn't have a 'gang' as such. She hung out with the nerds and the junkies both.

Time was running out.

***

Everything worked like clockwork. The police tried to dissuade him from paying the ransom, but he made his stand clear – the police could arrest the kidnappers after his daughter was safe at home.

At 4:00 PM, Sachin messaged him that the transfer money was ready in his wallet and the transfer could be initiated.

He sent a message to the kidnappers' WhatsApp number – "Money ready. Share details of sending Shravya back before starting transfer."

A message came back within five minutes – "Shravya will walk into her house between 5:30 and 6:00 PM."

This was followed by a video of Shravya. She was sitting at a table and in front of her was her favourite pizza. She seemed to be ok. She was not smiling, but was helping herself to the pizza.

Vinay showed the video to Bharati. They heaved a collective sigh of relief.

The police team quickly took this video also to the forensics team.

At 4:10 PM, a WhatsApp message came –

"Initiate transfer now.

<Wallet ID>
As soon as the transfer is complete, Shravya will walk.
Tell the police to stop wasting their time."

The police had set up a Web WhatsApp[4] on a police computer to monitor the chat. They immediately started trying to get whatever details they could about the recipient wallet.

***

Vinay called Aryan and updated him. Aryan was also some sort of a computer whiz. Something to do with security and all. Aryan heard Vinay out and then said calmly, "Vinay, most likely, this wallet would be based outside India. We won't be able to do anything. Our only hope is to catch the kidnappers physically. Please negotiate with the kidnappers to let you come and pick up Shravya from a physical location."

Vinay sent a message, "Can I pick up my daughter?"

The reply came, "No. End of chatting."

Vinay called Sachin and asked him to initiate the transfer immediately. He did not want anything to happen to Shravya. He told the police team – politely but firmly, "I have co-operated. I have shared information. But now, my child will first come home, and then we will talk. Please understand my situation."

The police had no option but to agree.

The minutes after that were tense. The transfer itself would take no more than ten minutes. The message from the kidnappers should have come, but it didn't.

At about 5:40 PM, Shravya's phone, which had been put on surveillance, suddenly started getting a signal. The location of the phone was near their house. It was moving towards the house.

Vinay and Bharati made it to their house in a mad scramble. They entered five minutes after the phone had entered the house. Fearing the worst, they opened the door of the house and rushed in, screaming Shravya's name.

"What????" Shravya screamed back. She had made her way to her bedroom and was washing up when her parents entered the house.

"Are you OK, beta?" they rushed to her.

"Huh? What would happen to me? The phone got all weird, though. No signal at all. I even had to take an auto home. Couldn't book Uber."

Vinay and Bharati stared at her in shock.

"Shravya, you were kidnapped, beta.. did they mess with your brain? Did they hypnotise you?"

"What are you guys talking about? I was out with some friends! We made the plan after school today and then my phone just wouldn't work. So, I couldn't send you a message. But since my curfew doesn't start till 6:00 PM, I figured I would be safe so long as I got home by six. What kidnapping? What nonsense! I was watching a movie!"

Vinay opened his phone to show her the chat. Disappearing messages had been turned on. There was nothing to show.

Vinay hugged his daughter really, really tight. Thank Goodness!

***

At night, after tucking the kids in, Vinay decided to call Aryan and share the details with him. Earlier, he had only sent one text – 'She is home.'

Aryan was awake and waiting for his call.

When he heard that Shravya had never been kidnapped, he was also nonplussed. How could this be?

He quickly took out a pen and paper and started making notes.

"Vinay, does anyone else in her friends' group have the same service provider as Shravya?"

"Yes. A child called Meenal uses the same service."

"Did she have a service outage too?"

"Errm, I don't know."

"Never mind, I will have this checked. It's possible that only Shravya's phone was hacked and jammed. But if she was at the movies, who was in those videos? A look alike? A cousin, or a sister?"

"No one we know, Aryan. No one in the family looks like Shravya that much. Besides, it was her favourite pizza."

"Is there ANYONE who knows her curfew time?"

"No one we know of, Aryan. This is very specific information. I am sure we don't share it randomly. But her friends might know."

Aryan was quiet for a few seconds. "Does your daughter have a social media account? Was she recently interviewed by someone about parents disciplining teens?"

"She is active on all her social media, yes. She has a YouTube channel, a Facebook account, an Insta account, Snapchat account, everything. But she only has her friends there. About the interview, let me ask Bharati."

Bharati vaguely remembered that some email had come asking kids to fill up a survey on small things like curfew times, whether they are allowed to go out alone with friends, sleepover policy, etc. It was a couple of months ago, if memory served her right.

"OK. Thanks Vinay. You've had a rough day. You rest. Leave this with me."

***

A week later, Aryan called Vinay, "I have the answers, Vinay. Would you like to know how it happened?"

"What a question to ask, Aryan! I am dying to know how this was pulled off! Both kids and Bharati have not left home without PSO[5]s since the day it happened, but we are all totally lost. Before how, I want to know **what** exactly happened!"

Aryan chuckled, "It is interesting, yes. Why don't the three of you come by later today? Office will be just fine. See you soon!"

***

At the right time, Vinay, Bharati, and Shravya were sitting in Aryan's office.

"Shravya beta, your dad has put PSOs to accompany you wherever you go. But that is more or less irrelevant to this case. The leak is not there at all. Would you like to know what happened?"

Shravya nodded.

Aryan continued, "The three things that led to your fake kidnapping, let's just call it that for now, were –

A. The survey you answered without knowing the person behind the survey.

B. Your videos on your social media, and

C. Your "Wait-for-It" kind of posts on Insta. These posts get you a lot of engagement, because excitement builds up for the followers. So, all content creators make a lot of these."

Bharati was staring at Aryan, "But how can someone fake kidnap her through her social media, and take that ransom? How??"

Aryan smiled, "When you break it down, this case has only three main elements. One, that Shravya's phone was unreachable for some time – about 2.5 hours. Two, that you saw video evidence that manipulated you into paying a ransom within those 2.5 hours. Three, that the ransom was paid to a crypto wallet, so, following the money would be next to impossible.

So, essentially, this was not a physical crime at all. This was cybercrime.

We start with these three elements and trace them back to their cause – how was this done, and we come up with a complete picture of the crime.

They used her existing social media videos to make a set of deepfakes. Once the deepfakes were ready, they took her personal info like curfew time, acceptable range of absence, etc., from that fake survey. And then, they just had to wait for a time when her phone was going to be inaccessible for two hours.

They just needed those two hours to get the money from you. Shravya would not miss her phone in a movie and would not try to call you. They had to jam her phone, so it would appear to be out of network coverage. That would affect you, not her. Then, they needed to send you those deepfakes, and ensure that the delivery of the crypto was done within the two hours of the movie. That simple! Funny, isn't it?"

Vinay was staring at Aryan, clearly incredulous, "That simple? Train a deepfake, wait for the child to be in a movie, and blackmail the parents? Really? That's it?"

"Yeah," Aryan nodded.

"And they got away with it!? Please tell me there will be some justice!"

"Vinay, if my surmise is correct, they never set foot on Indian soil. The whole operation was conducted online, from a country that is far, far away from India.

A simple text message carried the script injection that would allow the hacker to jam the phone signal at will. Shravya would never get to know that such a script was there on her phone.

The deepfakes, we have already discussed.

The only thing left was the opportunity. That opportunity would have presented itself sooner or later. And it did. None of us thought to check her Instagram account. In fact, the time crunch made sure that we did not even think of her social media, email, or YouTube channel at all. We focused on her physical location."

***

Three very quiet people left the room that day.

***

PS: Since writing this story, this MO[6] has unfortunately been attempted.

People have also received phone calls stating that the child has been arrested by the police and deepfakes have been used to convince the parent about the arrest.

[1] This Indianism means – her phone is appearing switched off.

[2] For this story, a fictional crypto exchange.

[3] This information is usually called meta-data. Meta-data means data about data. It is embedded automatically in most files.

[4] An application that shows a phone's WhatsApp messages on the computer screen.

[5] Personal Security Officers

[6] MO: Modus Operandi

CHAPTER FIVE

Brtdr.xyz

"And.... Send!" Bella did her trademark sign off flourish while pressing the send button, as always.

In this day and age of instant advice on tap, people still waited to hear from her.

She only posted two answers a day, but the views on those two answers made up 20% of the total traffic on the website. Not a mean feat by any standard. No wonder brtdr.xyz paid her so well and did everything to retain her.

Bella, born Bela Ravindran, moved to the USA like a lot of people from her state, to complete her master's degree in computer science.   Admissions were not easy then, and every win was celebrated by the whole community. She still remembered the sendoff party thrown in her honour. The entire neighbourhood was there.

Bela had come to the Land of Dreams. She got help from the seniors who had travelled before her. She completed her Masters degree successfully, graduated (how proud her Amma and Appa[1] were that day), and got a job.

That went on for five years – job, marriage, and a divorce. At the end of five years, Bela found herself divorced, alone, and laid off.

It was the season of layoffs. She just happened to be on the wrong list at the wrong time. That's how it was for literally hundreds of folks like her. In some cases, like hers, the person losing the job was also the sole breadwinner for the family.

Desperate times, as they say, call for desperate measures. While browsing, she bumped into this website – brtdr.xyz. Random strangers could share their problems and offer advice to each other. Just the thing she needed.

Pretty soon, she was addicted – spending hours on the website – venting out her own frustrations and giving advice to others.

***

"I am here to confess." The voice was calm. The speaker was standing straight. Not tall, but straight enough. Her hair looked matted. At any rate, they were open and not tied up or styled in any way. She was dressed in a loose one-piece western dress.

Arundhati, the lady constable, got up very quickly. Something about the tone was sinister. In a police station, one rarely heard the words, "I am here to confess" voluntarily. From women, even less so.

"Please come this way." Arundhati pointed to a room to her left.

Later, Arundhati's boss would praise her for this moment of poise and equanimity. Probably, this one moment of poise made all the difference to the case.

In the room, the lady started by saying that her name was Swapna. She was the survivor of fifteen years of domestic abuse – physical, financial, sexual, and emotional.

Being an orphan, she had no one to go to – a fact well understood and exploited by her husband, Nagesh. Nagesh wooed her softly for over four months, whispering into her ears how good-looking she was and how little his life meant without her. After her parents' death, the relatives had given her only shark-like bites to eat into her inheritance. No love. She was an easy prey.

They married within six months of being introduced. And she was put to work the very next day.

Nagesh was a mathematical genius in his own way. During the day, she was a teacher in a government school. This ensured job security, minimal work, and pension after retirement. Also, access to free health and medical facilities. By night, she was a worker in a very different industry. This ensured highest revenue per minute of time spent working. Sure, the work was dangerous, but Nagesh wasn't the one getting hurt.

This way, he maximized her earning potential. When not playing one of these two roles, she was, obviously, his default housekeeper and bartender.

And this was the hell that Swapna suffered for two years before breaking down in front of a colleague one day. The colleague, Shanti, was shocked and didn't know what to say. Most of them did face some kind of domestic abuse, but many of the girls these days were able to save themselves by threatening divorce. No one wanted to divorce a government employee. It was tough to become one (government jobs have the toughest selection criteria), and tougher still to find one worth marrying.

Shanti advised Swapna to meet an NGO lady. The NGO lady counselled her and threatened Nagesh. Things got better for a fortnight or so. Then, slowly, they began again. In innocuous ways. "Won't you get me a drink, the queen of my life?", "Who will I share a drink with, if not the one who rules my heart? All my thoughts are about you. All my dreams are yours."

Then, they slowly became sinister. Until, six months later, she was in the same hell all over again.

She blamed herself, of course. But didn't know how to break this cycle with Nagesh.

After nine years of this perennial cycle, everyone, including herself, just gave up. She surrendered to her fate.

The pattern perpetuated.

"So, what changed today?" Arundhati asked gently.

"There's this website. My friend told me about it. I go there to just vent. We can just talk to strangers, get advice, give advice, just speak our heart out. It's all anonymous. No one knows anyone else. I found this to be a very safe space where I could really say what was happening with me.

On this website, there is this feature – Bella's Advice Column. Bella picks up any two posts and shares her advice on them. Bella's advice is usually spot on. It is very specific. It tells the person what to do, how to do it, and when to do it. Like, it's as if a guide is standing there talking to you.

So many people have followed Bella's advice and their life has changed. Whether it is doing simple things like melatonin to fall asleep, or bigger things like community property in divorce cases, Bella is very real in what's possible and what's not, and very helpful.

I have been writing to Bella for advice for years now. Never got accepted.

Last week, Bella finally featured my problem.

I followed her advice."

"What was her advice?"

"The only way out of this mess is to kill my husband. Nothing else. Just kill him. If I want to live my life in peace, even inside a prison, that life would be better than what I am going through now."

Arundhati wanted to gasp. But didn't. She repeated slowly,   "Bella...   told...   you...

to...kill...your.....husband.....and....go....to...prison?"

"Yes."

"And....you.....followed....that....advice.....to.....a.....T?"

"Yes."

"Why? You could have run away. You didn't even need to kill. You could have divorced the fellow!"

"I tried the divorce route. You, madam, know what hell it is for a woman seeking divorce from a man who refuses. You make women go from family counselling to father judges who advise us to "adjust". You never have that advice for the husband. In the meantime, he would come and threaten me. Create public nuisance until no friend would have me in her house. No owner would rent a property to me.

You said I could have run away after killing him. But I could not have – for two reasons. One, you would have found me. Two, I don't want to live my life like a fugitive. I want to use my own documents and be my own self."

Arundhati had the presence of mind to show absolutely no emotional reaction whatsoever. She got a glass of water for Swapna to drink.

A police psychologist was summoned. She spoke with Swapna and certified that she was in a sound mental state and was making this confession voluntarily - no duress or influence – of people or substance.

While this was not necessary, the police officers thought it best to go through this before deploying any manpower on the case and sending police personnel to a so-called crime scene.

Once the formalities were completed, Arundhati sent a team to the crime scene.

The man was dead. No doubt about it. Other than that, the house was neat and clean. There wasn't that much to process at the crime scene, but they still took pictures and fingerprints.

The police team, led by Arundhati, took Swapna into custody, and made the case file with the chargesheet. This was an easy case.

***

ACP Rajeshwari Das was rocking her flexible office chair. Her face was titled upwards and the eyes were closed. This usually happened when she was thinking her way out of a tricky problem. The "Do Not Disturb" sign outside her door was on.

But the seats in front of her were not empty. One of them was occupied by Jatin. Jatin was Swapna's lawyer. Swapna, who had confessed and requested a speedy trial, was not granted her wish. A government lawyer was defending her. That government lawyer was Jatin.

After meeting Swapna a few times, Jatin had been convinced that he did not want this woman to suffer for a murder that was inevitable.

The poisoning was deliberate and pre-meditated, so he could not argue insanity or self-defence.

He then used that brilliant lawyer brain and filed for "influence". The columnist called Bella had a position of influence as far as the subject (Swapna) was concerned. She had used that influence to not just encourage, but almost coerce Swapna into committing an illegal act – by saying that this was the ONLY way for her to live peacefully. Not only that, it must also be noted that prior to Bella's "suggestion", the idea of murder had not occurred to the person accused. It was neither her original intent, nor her idea. She had only been used as the execution device.

Therefore, the chargesheet must be modified to include the columnist who writes as Bella as the primary accused.

Swapna was under undue influence at the time of committing the murder. Further, Bella materially coerced the subject, Swapna, by indicating that this was "The only way" for her to live peacefully.

Arundhati had forwarded the submission to ACP Das.

ACP Das had to admire the creativity of the young man. She wanted this case disposed of quickly. In the interest of time, she asked her assistant to reach out to Jatin and call him for a meeting.

***

After listening to Jatin's thoughts, ACP Das was inclined to agree with him. A battered woman anyway loses half her mind every day. Added to that was the fact that Swapna had tried every other choice – separation, divorce, police case for domestic violence, family counselling, everything. This man was making it impossible for her to lead a normal life. To such a person, the idea that murder was the only way to live peacefully, would appear to be logical and true.

And it was also true that prior to this advice, Swapna had never considered murdering Nagesh. The idea was planted in her mind for the first time by that advice columnist. The specificity of the plan had made it possible for her to execute the said plan. Both the idea and the method were given by the columnist. Swapna executed it, presumably under undue influence.

"Madam," Jatin was still speaking, "This is the same as a woman who kills her children under the influence of some tantrik[2]. We also charge the tantrik under the same Section 302[3]. This case is identical. These advice columnists are the new tantriks."

"Where does this advice columnist live?"

"We don't know, ma'am. The Whois entry[4] of the website itself is also masked. We know nothing about where this Bella is from. But that alone should not stop us from making her a co-accused."

"Jatin, the difference between the tantrik and Bella is this – we have jurisdiction over the tantrik. The main reason you are doing this is to get bail for Swapna, no? You apply for bail. I see no reason for us to contest it. She is a good person. Don't think she will go out and do anything stupid. Let this case be. Don't weaken it unnecessarily with this Bella nonsense. I promise to think about this some more. You have raised an important point. But in this case, I am not changing the chargesheet. Sorry."

ACP Das closed the file with finality.

"Madam, I am not asking to add Bella only for bail. I ask because Swapna will not be the only woman going to these anonymous websites to vent. Do think about what I am saying. You are in a state that prides itself on its track record on prosecuting digital crime. Isn't this also a form of digital crime? Inducing murder, sitting far away from the hands of the law? Do think, madam. You may not be able to prosecute this columnist. But at least you will send a message across."

ACP Das knew, even in that moment, that the decision was not hers to make. She would have to consult her seniors.

***

The seniors did get involved – all the way to the CM, who was the darling of the tech Moguls. He dined with them at industry events, gently cajoling them to invest more money in his state – renting offices, providing jobs (creating a market for thousands of homes made and sold by his construction company).

When he heard about the case and the request of the police to file for getting the identity information of the columnist and then making her a co-accused in the trial, he kept quiet for more than a minute. Saying no would mean antagonising the police – never a good idea. Saying yes would mean raised eyebrows at the industry dinner this Wednesday.

"Let me get back to you." He said to the state police chief.

***

Swapna, meanwhile, had used her bail time to log back on to the site and write on the forums how she followed Bella's column and was now accused of murder. The forums were divided – some ridiculed her for not using her judgement on something as basic as "Not killing someone", while some others blamed Bella for suggesting something that was clearly illegal, in every part of the world. "Does Bella have a conscience at all?" Many posters asked.

The editorial team of brtdr.xyz had reached out to Bella, demanding an explanation. Now that they knew that the person had followed the advice (like everyone before her), they had to cover their backsides against any legal and user backlash. So far, they were not doing a very good job.

Bella was stunned. Her column had advised someone to kill their husband, and they had done it?

At first, she did not believe it. When the *brtdr* team showed her the post, she read through her own advice and was amazed at the specificity of it. The answer was worded in a very persuasive manner. Anyone reading this, even Bella, would have agreed with the answer. Now she knew why people always followed the advice given in her column.

"Is there a legal liability for me, personally?" she asked Stella, her contact from *brtdr*.

"My dear, the legal liability is all yours. We publish a disclaimer, see, that we are only intermediaries. The advice being sought, and given, and any liability arising out of actions therefrom, belongs completely to the two parties involved – you and the poster. Having said that, we won't be able to avoid the backlash, I'm sure. I would suggest you get a lawyer. In the meantime, I am sending you an email, terminating our relationship with immediate effect. I'm sorry, Bella. You really were our rock star." Stella signed off.

Bella's head was spinning. She didn't know what to do next.

***

Brtdr thought that once it released a statement terminating its relationship with Bella, people would move on within weeks, if not days. But the opposite happened. The user community started shrinking rapidly. Within two weeks, *brtdr's* traffic was down 50%. Average active users per day dropped even more quickly – as many as 60% of the daily active users abandoned the website.

Brtdr had a business problem on its hands. The other internet forums were quick to pick it up as a 'case study' and discuss it threadbare.

It had no idea about the legal problem - yet.

***

Jatin reached out to a few media outlets on his own. Even though it was illegal to discuss sub-judice cases, he made the leak – discreetly. The journalists would report as if they had picked up the story on international forums.

The story of a columnist sitting in a first world country influencing a mentally battered person in India to commit murder, was too good to pass up. It was national news within two days. Opinion pieces flew thick and fast, and TV debates soared. Everyone was unanimous in demanding criminal action against the columnist – wherever they may be physically located.

That is how someone in Delhi read about the case. A few phone calls later, someone from the Union ministry got involved. The ambassador of the first world country was called and "encouraged" to share the details of the website owners, as a "small gesture of goodwill."

The Ambassador made some enquiries and realised, much to his relief, that the said columnist was of Indian origin. Promptly, the personal details of the columnist were passed on to the Indian government.

****

"So, help me understand. This is your column?"

"Yes."

"You write this advice, and you did not know that you have advised someone to commit murder, with very specific steps?"

"For the last six months, I have not been the one writing that column. I use AutoChat – an AI driven LLM[5], to write out the answers. Earlier, I would check them. But they are so good that now I don't even read. I just copy paste the answer from the chat window to the email and send. No one else knows this."

Jim stared. If there was a word for being speechless, he needed it now.

"Your column answers are written by AutoChat?"

"Yes. I am a computer science graduate. I learnt prompt engineering and then invested in a professional generative AI product for writing. I give the prompts for style, etc. But now the engine pretty much knows my style based on user ID, and is fairly automatic."

"So, why are you here?"

"The thing is, if I am sued, I would like to sue the makers of AutoChat for releasing a public solution before it has been tested for safety. If their product is making a kill recommendation, it has obviously not been tested for safety, right?"

"As it turns out, madam, they have gone public with the information that the solution has biases and is not tested for safety."

"I am a professional, paying user of AutoChat. The 'service' being offered by AutoChat AI Solution is writing. If the writing is not reliable or even safe, what am I paying for? Why is this a commercial product?

If any liability comes to me, that is directly attributable to the work product generated by a paid product, that liability has to be passed on to the creators of the product."

"Madam, that is how it would work in the normal course of things. But in this case, the 'service' you have bought is flawed, and openly so. Therefore, you assume the risk. I am sorry, there is no legal case here. I could represent you if the website sued you for a subpar or potentially damaging work product. But we could not represent you on a case against Big Tech."

A sly smile played on Bella's lips. "What do you think will happen if I go public with the fact that this advice column was written by AutoChat? I have lost my job already. What's to lose? It is one thing to say a product has not been tested fully for biases. Quite another to cause a death. Do you think enterprise customers would still pay for integrating AutoChat as the base LLM in their own enterprise chatbots? After all, how much editing oversight can an enterprise provide in its own chatbot? What if the solution recommends to a user that the only way to deal with an abusive boss is to kill them?"

Jim stared, for the second time, at the woman sitting in front of him. This time, his jaw openly dropped.

"Madam, I am a corporate lawyer. I have no expertise in this kind of case. Maybe you should speak to our criminal law team. I will have a partner sent out shortly, if you would just wait here for some time."

And Jim exited that room as quickly as he could. Any partner in the criminal team, he knew, would be more than willing to be in that room. An actual case on criminal liability of AI! And theirs would be one of the first firms to handle it!

***

Unfortunately, that didn't go as planned. The deliberations fell flat. Big Tech refused to assume any liability. No settlement was offered.

But someone (possibly from the law firm, but who knows?) leaked to an online AI news website the details of the case. They reached out to Bella immediately, offering her some money to share her story with them.

In tears, Bella came on video and shared how she was one of the first adopters of new tech. She had become a paying customer of AutoChat as soon as a paid version was released. She told the story as is, blaming AutoChat for the murder and for her own loss of livelihood. "My only fault is that I trusted the solution. A solution I was told to trust and a commercial solution that I was paying for. But this is not about me. This is about what the future of humanity will be if we allow this to go unchecked. I did not provide human oversight. But this AI solution will soon form the backbone of hundreds of chatbot solutions in corporate America and global corporations. What human oversight will they provide to each answer going out of the solution? Who is responsible if this AI solution tells an employee that the only way out of their predicament is suicide? Or murder? Or mass shooting? After my experience, that doesn't sound so impossible, does it? Their solution for an abusive husband is murder. Can you imagine the impact of that on our American society? On American families?"

The response was immediate. And widespread. Corporate America shut down every single chatbot project that included this LLM solution. Other LLM solutions came under the scanner too. "What if?" became the national question.

Like the flu, it spread – first to Canada, then Europe, then Southeast Asia. Pretty soon, the lawyer who had offered no settlement to Bella did not look so smart to his employers any more.

***

The murder case ran on in India. Jatin placed the facts of the case again in front of the judge. The sessions court decided in a record time of four months. Swapna was given life imprisonment, but parole application could be allowed in due course.

Jatin convinced her that she should be out in two, at most three years. Swapna looked at him and smiled, "And go where, Jatin ji? Who is waiting for me outside? No house, no money, no family. This is my life now. I am happy."

But it was not the prison sentence that made headlines. It was the quote in the judgement.

"We are possibly looking at the first crime attributable to the influence of AI. This should serve as a strict warning to all of us in general, but the architects of AI in particular. AI optimises outcomes in a rational, inhuman manner. What is to stop AI from recommending mass culling of humans in the event of a drought, famine, or, say, a global pandemic? That is the mathematically optimal solution, but is it the right one?"

***

The US Congress invited the CEOs of the top four AI companies for a Congressional hearing.

The CEOs admitted that the product probably should not have been offered as a commercial solution just yet, but denied any deliberate wrongdoing. They maintained that they acted 'to the best of their ability' but were not in a position to provide any guarantees in the foreseeable future.

All commercial AI LLM solutions that provided chat output were immediately taken off the market.

Big Tech was not happy, of course. Every day without revenue is a loss-making day. More importantly, LLMs were, so far, free of any regulation. This Congressional hearing meant that future LLM AI solutions were likely to face some sort of standards requirement.

Brtdr.xyz received a legal notice.

Instead of trying to fight the Big Tech behemoth, they decided to shut shop.

Brtdr closed the website a month after receiving the legal notice. All employees were paid the highest severance the company could manage – the CEO personally saw to that. Thousands of users who were still loyal, wrote heartfelt posts about what the website had meant to them.

***

In her house, Bela Ravindran sat with a friend. Two cups of coffee were on the table, and there was silence.

"Say something, Bela. Anything. What comes to your mind first when you think of everything that's happened? Is it your job loss? How will you earn again? What will your family think of you? That poor woman? What is it? Just tell me!"

"Only this, Sharada – Who, really, is responsible for that man's death? His wife was under undue influence. I relied on a professional writing service. And the creators of that AI? Who, really?"

[1] Mom and dad

[2][2] Tantrik – Magic healer

[3] Now section 103 of the Bhartiya Nyaya Sanhita – India's new criminal law. In the old Indian Penal Code, Section 302 applied to murder.

[4] Whois entry tells us who owns a website, their address, etc.

[5] LLM – Large Language Model. These AI programs are fed on a vast amount of conversational data and are then used to create chatbots like ChatGPT and others.

CHAPTER SIX

The Ambria Trialogue

Eva looked at the boarding cards. As a business class purser, she was used to meeting important people as her passengers. But she had never seen Indian officials board the business class of an American airline. All Indian officials had to fly charter or Indian Air – India's national carrier. They had strict rules about the use of devices, where they could or could not show their identity documents, and in which public spaces they could or could not talk – even for private travel. So, this was rather surprising. But truth be told, Air America was far more luxurious than the Indian national airline, so the officials could hardly be blamed for preferring the most luxurious airline in the world. 'Maybe they got a minister to sign off on the budget or something', she chuckled to herself.

The guests settled in. They were not particularly demanding. The flight was good.

***

AS, the Ambrian Member of Parliament (MP), welcomed the guests warmly into his home. A part of his house was set up to host them. The guests and AS held several closed-door discussions over the next few days.

The Ambrian Prime Minister was very happy with AS.

AS had pulled off a coup d'éclat by bringing Indian officials and Indian separatists to the table. The Prime Minister was anyway sick of these nonstop anti-India protests in his country. But because most of his funders (and ministers) were of Indian origin, he had no choice but to allow these 'democratic protests'. With this, he hoped, that the headache would reduce somewhat as India and the separatists spoke about their issues.

Within a fortnight, the contingent returned to India via the same airline they had used to fly in. Their mission was successful.

***

Three months later, the Ambrian PM stood in Parliament and thundered, "Our sovereignty is under attack, but we will not allow it. No nation, however strong, has a right to conduct a targeted attack on our soil. Indian agents have killed an Ambrian citizen in a targeted assassination on our soil."

Two days later, the United States made a 'statement' – "India must not subvert the sovereignty of any nation. We encourage India to fully co-operate with the Ambrian authorities in the investigation of this incident, which we have reason to believe, was a political assassination."

***

AS made a hurried visit to the Prime Minister's office. He was not just surprised at the allegation (he had heard about it for the first time in the Parliament!), he was also miffed that no evidence had been shared with him, nor was he involved in the investigation. Was he also under suspicion? Was this a ploy to unseat him by his political rivals? What was going on here?

AS was kept waiting for two hours – a far cry from the day when, just two weeks ago, he had been ushered in as the only MP to meet the President of Drukain who happened to be visiting Ambria.

When the Prime Minister did meet him, he was not particularly warm. But AS was on a mission. "How did we know that my guests were the ones who did the assassination?" he asked.

The Prime Minister looked at him. There was a flicker of uncertainty, and then, as if he had made up his mind, the Prime Minister took a deep breath and invited AS to sit down.

"You do know about the UAUA intelligence alliance – USA – Ambria – UK – Australia. I was given this information by the UAUA alliance. They sent me the passports, the identity documents used to buy the gun, the travel itineraries, the cell phones used while in US and Ambria – everything. It was all from the top-notch intelligence agency in the world. They were hoodwinking you – and me – the whole time."

AS did not have time to circumlocute, "Am I under the scanner too? Under suspicion?"

The PM did not flinch, "Neither. We know you were on the up and up. These guys, like I said, hoodwinked all of us. You included."

***

The matter reached the United Nations.

Ambria and USA made almost daily statements – both in their local press, and in the UN General Assembly, about the importance of mutual respect and absolute holding up of the sovereignty of a nation.

Indians on social media tried reminding the Americans that they had quite respected the sovereignty of Pakistan at Abbottabad[1], but the pressure was building up for real. The UN Secretary General received the largest funding from a single country – USA, and while members differed on the veracity of claims, it was important to toe the line where the largest donor was involved.

The Indian envoy to the UN was a competent man. Even so, the debonair foreign minister of India was called. He made a very impressive speech at the UN General Assembly, highlighting that the man who had been killed was a known terrorist and Ambria should worry more about giving refuge to terrorists than about any so-called covert act that India had done on its soil.

***

In India, RAW[2] was in a ruffle. No Indian agency had even ordered this hit, much less executed it. How was such a baseless allegation coming from such a friendly country?

The UN Secretary General himself mediated and asked Ambria to share its evidence with the intelligence agency of India.

Ambria shared its evidence – 5 Indian officers – 2 foreign service officers and 3 RAW agents, had travelled to Ambria in their personal capacity – on a commercial airplane. In Ambria, they procured a weapon from the neighbouring USA. Then, they used that gun to eliminate a leading separatist leader with roots in India. It was all there – their travel tickets, their local taxi, their trip to USA, their purchase receipt, their local burner cells in Ambria and USA, everything. They stayed with an Indian-origin Ambrian MP, pretending to be there to resolve the issue with the separatists. Unknown to their host, they had procured the weapon and executed the assassination, while blindsiding everyone with their 'peace overtures'.

It was simply unforgivable.

India checked. They were stupefied. None of these 5 officers had travelled to Ambria any time in the past year.

These documents were shared with Ambria – the attendance sheets of the officials, their presence in India confirmed by their appearance in meetings held physically in their offices. No travel documents or even leaves had been approved for these officers. They were in office, in the presence of hundreds of colleagues. Their cell phones were in India. Their physical presence was in India. There had been no travel – personal or official. There had been no leaves of absence. Their passports were also not stamped.

Now it was Ambria's turn to be surprised. The 5 officers had used diplomatic channel, so they literally went unscreened. The Ambrian MP had sponsored their visas, and they already held diplomatic passports. But they HAD come, interacted, met with some separatist leaders, made placatory noises on behalf of India, and had ensured further, ongoing talks.

The Ambrian Prime Minister called the MP who had sponsored their diplomatic visas. He was shown the passports sent by the Indians. He looked at them and confirmed the name, photographs, everything. Then, at one of the pictures, he paused. "This is not the Rama Krishna who visited me." He said, perplexed.

The Ambrian Secret Service, which was anyway angry at the political establishment for keeping them out of the loop on these 'very sensitive' talks, had deployed Harold, a special officer, to take these passport copies to AS. When he heard these words from AS, he asked AS to look at all the five passports carefully. AS noted that all the other faces looked similar, though after so many months, he could hardly be expected to certify that they were identical. But Rama Krishna did look slightly different.   Comparison with the photos shared by US intelligence did not help either. They were from CCTV footage, meaning they were approximate rather than accurate. Why they can make telescopes that see stars that are light years away but not CCTVs that show faces that are five meters away - is a mystery for another day.

Harold looked at the passport copies received from India. Then, he looked at the visa copy got from the Ambrian Immigration authorities. The passport number is typically punched in on the side of the passport booklet. He looked carefully at that and found that the passport numbers of the passports shared by the Indians and the passports received in Ambria were different. **In short, one person, two passports.**

Usually, fake passports are made for short term missions. But NEVER with the original identity of the agent. Meaning, if Agent A has to travel to Russia for some work, it would be basic SOP[3] to make them a fake passport. But that fake passport would have the name B. It would have a different address, and so on. Never would the real identity of A be disclosed for a fake passport.

Since India and Ambria had been friendly countries before this, Harold did have a few friends and connections. He reached out to one of them and told him about the two different passport numbers.

The Indian intelligence officer (for the sake of nostalgia, let's call him Vijay, because his real name cannot be shared) took in this piece of information. Fake passports for missions were obviously the norm, but in this case, he knew that India had ordered no hit and was now being accused on the global stage very deliberately. This was a joint war of diplomacy and intelligence.

This was turning out to be more sinister than they had originally thought. It was not just a case of fake passports. These fake passports were based on identity theft of Indian intelligence officers, and **now**, RAW had something bigger to worry about.

So, in short, five people of unknown origin had got fake passports based on the identities of Indian senior officers, travelled commercial on these fake passports, and executed a hit. Like ghosts, they had vanished. Who could be behind this, and why? Who were these people?

***

The Ambrian Secret Service shared the copies of the passports with the Indian authorities. The Indian government found something shocking. All these diplomatic passports had been issued within the last year. They had no history of travel to any place other than Ambria. They had been issued within two months of each other.

Obviously, someone inside the country was conspiring to create an international embarrassment for India. The plot had been crafted over months. This meant that the objective could not be as simple as accusing India on the international stage. This issue was going to be huge. The party was just getting started.

***

Vijay got a call from his boss (whom we will call Jai, because his name also cannot be revealed). There was a specific instruction – Vijay was to reach out to Rao sir. Rao sir was a retired RAW officer who also had experience in international diplomacy. More than that, he was sharp. Really sharp.

Vijay had to bring Rao sir up to speed on everything that had happened so far – Everything. Then, Vijay was to ask Rao sir for his advice. This case was going to be solved by Rao sir's brain and Vijay's hands. Everyone else, including Jai, was to be on need-to-know basis[4] only.

After he had heard him out, Rao sir sat back, closed his eyes, and just remained that way for five minutes. After that, he opened his eyes, "I am going to sum up my understanding so far. You confirm or correct, ok?"

"Yes, sir."

"Step 1: Some persons start to recce our intelligence officers to copy their looks, mannerisms, etc. a few months before the day of assassination, which we will call T.

Step 2: Fake passports are made using the actual identities of these officials.

Step 3: Five unknown people travel to Ambria, do a hit, and come back. They fly commercial and leave lots of breadcrumbs on the way – buying their own gun, getting caught on CCTV, staying at the house of a political host, and so on.

Step 4: Two months after T, the Ambrian Prime Minister gets some evidence from UAUA alliance, but I think we can safely assume it was USA, to prove that these five Indian officers were behind the hit.

Step 5: The Ambrian PM asks his secret service to check the submission of the US. The submission is obviously found to be true. The Ambrian PM starts the s^&*storm by making a public accusation in the Parliament, no less.

Step 6: Two days later, the US jumps in with global statements about the murder. They force the UN to get involved and put India on the defensive.

Step 7: Our diplomats and foreign minister are defending the salvos, but so far, it's a growing offensive.

Have I got it ok so far?"

Vijay was clearly impressed, "Sir, you have summarized so much information in so few words. Now I know why Jai sir asked me to reach out to you." Rao sir brushed aside the compliment and went back to his meditation pose before speaking again.

"Now, I have some questions. If you have a notepad, start writing. What you know the answer to, tell me now. What you don't know, find out.

One, what is the political status of AS, the MP who hosted these guys? If you can, reach out to this person and ask him how the Indians got in touch with him. Who contacted him? What did they say? How did they convince him to bypass the regular dialogue channels and host this secret meeting?

Two, how did the US know to keep an eye on these five gents? Why did they keep an eye on them? Literally thousands of Indians on Ambrian visa cross the border every day and hundreds of guns are sold every day in the US. Why were these guys on the radar?

Three, from our passport office, find the original application files of the fake passports. What are the ID and police verification documents on those files? Bring me the CCTV footage from the Passport Seva Kendra. If possible, also get me the agents who worked on completing this passport applications. That is where the key is – the successful identity theft of our folks."

"Sure, sir." Vijay responded. Then, he drank the glass of water offered to him and left.

***

Just two days later, Vijay was back at Rao sir's house.

Sir, the MP who hosted the five ghosts is ok. He is no longer the darling of the PM, but neither is he worse off. We did reach out to him. He mentioned that he was contacted through an official government of India email ID. All calls and discussions were held via internet calls – for 'security', according to the Indian officials.

These people clearly mentioned to him that they are RAW officials and RAW wants to help him, so he might become a minister in Ambria *and* a friend of India. The MP thought it was a good strategy. The plan they told him is bizarre:

They would come to Ambria. The popular spiel would be that they are coming for peace talks with the separatists. But actually, they would help by taking out a person who is now becoming a liability to the separatist movement. The Ambrian PM would love AS for hosting peace talks, and the separatists would love him for taking care of a liability. Of course, if any peace deal had actually been struck, that would have been a bonus. It was to be a win-win for everyone. He agreed easily.

Everything went to plan and the outcome was exactly as predicted."

"So, the Ambrian MP knew all along that these people were going to kill a separatist?"

"Appears so, sir. Yes."

"I want to see a copy of the first email he got – from the India government email ID."

"Sorry, sir?"

"Do you have a copy now?"

"Errm.. yes sir..." a confused Vijay looked for the printout in his folder and handed it over.

Rao sir looked at it and laughed out loud.

"This email ID is rajesh.kumar@india.gov."

"Yes, sir?"

"The domain of government of India is gov.in, not india.gov. This email was never sent from any Indian government office. Their plan was to make him think that it was coming from an Indian official, and to ensure that he never talks to any official Ambrian channels about this email."

Vijay was dumbstruck. Then, he cleared his throat.

"We have no idea why the US kept an eye on these people. The US secret service is being very rude and unco-operative.

I have the original passport applications. As you can see, they all have a government issued ID attached as proof of identity and as proof of residence. The officers in question swear that they have never shared these ids with anyone. They have no idea how this happened. And frankly, neither do we."

Rao sir sat back in his favourite chair again.

"From now on, make no contact with the Ambrians or the US secret service. Focus on these passports. I want you to check if any other Indian diplomat's passport has been issued in the last 2 years. Usually, these operations begin with a long list[5]. So, for 5 operatives, they would have got at least 8 passports made.

I want you to go over the cell phone records of these officers for the 3 months leading up to the passport application. I don't think they were compromised in any way, but one can never be too sure."

With that, the meeting ended.

***

"Vijay, see na[6]!" Neela called out from her computer. At this point, Vijay did not want to see anything, but Neela's sweet voice was always hard to ignore. They complemented each other perfectly. Vijay was in the dark business of espionage, while Neela was in the sweetest possible job – a kindergarten teacher – bringing sunshine and joy to young hearts every morning. No wonder Vijay cherished each interaction with his wife.

Today, she was ordering a new saree on Nile, the world's most popular e-commerce website.

Vijay helped her choose a saree and got back to his paperwork. In the back of his mind, he realised that 90% of their lives were now dependent on American companies – phone, laptops, operating systems, cars, e-commerce, search engine, and ALL social media – everything was American. "If they pool their knowledge, between them, Google, Microsoft, and Meta can create a virtual avatar of every single Indian citizen." – this was the last stray thought in his head before he dived into the call records once more. This fishing expedition was going to be useless. He had full faith in the integrity of the officers.

****

Rao sir was waiting for him this time. Of course, he had been right – not eight, but nine passports of Indian RAW and IFS officers had been issued in the last two years.

"But how were these passports issued?"

"Sir, our process is to check the identity documents to ensure that they are correct. We don't check that no other passport is issued against these identity documents. That is the technology loophole that was exploited this time."

"Hmmm.. OK. Was anyone from the Passport Seva Kendra (PSK) involved?"

"Sir, we have looked extensively. No, they weren't. Our PSK followed the process correctly. The fake ID documents were very convincing."

"Then, my dear, the key question becomes – how were these ID documents obtained?

Also, I want you to go over the whereabouts of the lower order Ambrian embassy staff very carefully. The recruitment of our ghosts was not done by the Ambassador. It was done by spies masquerading as lower-level staff, even visa counter officials. They may even have preyed upon the strong need to be in Ambria. I also want you to do a similar thing with the US embassy."

"The US embassy? But why, sir?" Vijay was shocked.

"Because, I think, that the recruitment happened at the Ambrian embassy, but was governed from the US embassy." Rao sir signed off with a wink.

It made no sense to Vijay.

***

International pressure was escalating by the day. Jai reached out to Vijay and explained the importance of working fast and getting evidence.

This was why Vijay was back with Rao sir the very next day.

"Vijay, for you to get evidence, I need to know how they stole identities in India. It is not enough to say identities were stolen. It is important to prove how and by whom. On my own, I have checked. These people did not apply for a loan or credit card with any foreign bank. They did not send children to any fancy school or new school. They did not even stay at hotels – Indian or foreign. So, I am unable to figure out where the leak is from."

"Right sir. Let me check the linkages of staff at US and Ambrian embassies by tonight. It's a huge task, but I will get it done."

***

The next morning began with a blast. The US Ambassador, speaking to a political news website of the US, mentioned that relations with India might worsen within the next few weeks. The report was immediately denied by the US State Department.

While Vijay was in the middle of all this, Neela called out again, "Vijay...."

"Yes, Neela?" for once, Vijay's tone was terse.

"I need your help here please. I am not able to login into our Nile account."

"Try again after some time please."

"I have been trying for a week! Please help me out here!"

"You are as tech savvy as I am. How can I help?"

"Come, na!" Neela was back to her sweet self, and Vijay could not resist.

She was unable to generate the OTP[7] for her Nile account. The only help being offered was the Account recovery page. On that page, the message was that Neela needed to upload her govt issued ID proof to validate her account. Then, the account would be unlocked, and a new OTP could be generated.

"Neela, buy from another website please. We should not have to give our identity documents to online retailers."

"Arre! What is wrong with this? How will they verify your identity, na? This happened on Facenook also last month. I got locked out of my account. Then I had to upload an ID document to get my account back."

"You.. what??"

"Chill Vijay.. what will a million-dollar company do with your identity document? Your profession has just made you unnecessarily doubt everything. It's fine. Never mind, I will do this later." Neela left. She was running late for school.

"Shit!!" Vijay muttered under his breath. Was he really becoming unnecessarily suspicious? What would a US company do with his ID anyway? How will they even know that he has uploaded his ID document? Some small agent sitting possibly in India only will take a cursory look and approve the account.

By the time he reached office, international geopolitics and his mood were both better. Ambria had asked for a dialogue with India to resolve the ongoing issues.

***

At 11:00 AM, Rao sir was in Jai's office. If Vijay was surprised to see him, his expression did not betray that.

He was beckoned in and motioned to a chair. Then, Rao sir started speaking.

"Jai, I have to start by commending this young man, Vijay, for his diligence and intelligence. And now, we must get to the heart of the matter."

Vijay smiled to himself. Rao sir was not one to mince or waste words.

"You would have heard that Ambria is asking for a dialogue. That is why I am here. This analysis needs to reach the Ministry before they respond. This is not a dialogue. This is a trialogue – the Ambria trialogue.

The three parties of interest are – America, India, and Ambria, in that order.

The separatists were growing in Ambria for a long time anyway. It worked for both countries – India, because better that they should be in Ambria than in neighbouring Pakistan; and Ambria, because of the moneys that flowed in with these folks.

This is where a third party saw an opportunity.

The killing of the separatist in Ambria was a state executed murder. The murderers were recruited from Indians wanting to migrate to Ambria. The recruitment officer was from the Ambrian Embassy, but the operation was being directed from the American embassy. The recce was done by the five gents themselves. They then got special training here, in India, on copying the mannerisms et al, of the person concerned.

The weapons training was likely done in Pakistan. The entire song and dance was orchestrated in the US all through.

A big challenge was the identity documents of the long list. I think they would have tried everything – KYC from the bank, loan offer, even hacking into the NIC database to get their digital employee file, free holidays, et al. But nothing worked, as we already know.

And then, a very unique method was used to get their identity documents. Their Nile accounts were locked and the unlock process required them to submit a government issued ID for 'verification'. Typically, some 'glitch' would show 'document not uploaded'. The user would then upload a second ID document. This time, the ID would be accepted, and after a phone call, their Nile IDs would be unlocked.

That is how they got two government approved IDs that are needed for passport application. Once they had the details, they just had to create a fake version. The ID number and details needed to be identical to pass the Passport Seva Kendra document verification. They had to be sure to involve as few Indians as possible. Any leak would have cost them heavily.

Now, their plan was ready – nine passports, five trained volunteers, and a ready host who would sponsor diplomatic visa."

At this point, Rao sir turned to both of them, "Jai and Vijay, have your or your family member's Nile accounts been facing problems lately?"

Vijay's head was spinning. He took a glass of water and sat down.

Rao sir continued, "The next step was really easy. From here, everything was under American control – American airline, gun from America, CCTV cameras conveniently placed. No one asked them – how did you track these guys?

How did you know this separatist was going to be killed? How do you have intelligence inside Ambria? The UAUA body is to share intelligence, not to collect intelligence inside each other's countries.

The hit was executed. The hitmen flew back to India, complete with CCTV coverage, and within a day, vanished from Indian soil.

Then, as planned, they waited two months before giving evidence to the Ambrian PM. This ensured two things – one, no questions on how the evidence was available so soon. And two, all traces other than the ones they wanted to keep, could be wiped off cleanly. Time is a great luxury in espionage.

Part three of the plan begins now – international pressure on India begins and is intensified in the months to come. Honestly, I don't know what the endgame is. It could be political isolation of India, it could even be sanctions, which the US has not been able to put against India. On many fronts – but most notably Russia and Iran, India is exempt from the sanctions largely because of its political power on the global stage and its high moral stand. Take that stand away and India will not just lose face, it will also lose a lot of financial and military access."

Jai sat back in his chair, his brow deeply furrowed, "Is there any way to prove any of this?"

Rao sir smiled, "Only one. The email that was sent to AS, the Ambrian MP. It was sent from the ID ravi.kishan@india.gov. Now, the .gov domain can ONLY belong to a US government website. No one, anywhere else, can buy a .gov domain."

"Rao Sir, do you have any suggestion on how to manage this communication?" Vijay asked.

Rao sir nodded in the negative, "No. This is a bigger game than anything we have played earlier. In my time, India was a Soviet ally[8]. It's like we used to play Nationals and suddenly you guys are in the Olympics. This is a much bigger stage. You younger folks will be best suited to decide what to do."

***

The communication was sent to Ambria. Within a week, the Ambrian side proposed a joint investigation into the death.

USA tried to reach out to Ambria but was politely told that for its economy to work, Ambria needed the money coming from Indian immigrants. Therefore, Ambria would have to work with India and maintain cordial relations.

***

A few months later, Rai sir and Jai were at the India Club – a quiet club for retired bureaucrats.

"Why do you think they did it, the Americans?" Jai asked.

There was a twinkle in Rao sir's eyes. He didn't need to ask what. The Ambrian trialogue had easily been the biggest intelligence heist that they had worked on together.

"Anyone's guess. But mine is that India was growing too big for its boots. It needed to be cut to size."

"Just that?" Jai was incredulous.

"That's a big deal Jai. Cutting India to size was a big ask at that time. It was not an easy job. India had assumed de jure leadership of G20 and orchestrated the entry of 42 African countries to G20. It had assumed de facto leadership of what it called the Global South. India was responsible for stopping global trade in dollars in at least two important exchanges – India-UAE and India- Russia. The entire American economy is based on just one thing –

global trade being in dollars. India, my dear, was a serious, serious threat."

Jai took a sip of his chai, and gently smiled, "Some tailors are not as good as they think, no, sir?"

Rao sir said nothing. His smile, on the other hand, said everything.

[1] At Abbottabad in Pakistan, US Navy Seals stormed a house and killed Osama Bin Laden. He was wanted for the 2001 attacks on the World Trade Center in America. America conducted this attack without even letting Pakistani authorities know. Bin Laden's body was "buried at sea" meaning he was just thrown into the water. No evidence was ever shared, no intelligence, and the US never answered to anyone for doing this act inside Pakistani territory.

[2] Research and Analysis Wing – India's topmost intelligence agency for international operations.

[3] SOP – Standard Operating Procedure – a guided way of doing something specific that is well documented and is almost always followed.

[4] Need to know basis means that every member of a team is only given the information that they need to know to complete their work.

[5] A long list is the first set of options for a decision. Some items from this are eliminated to arrive at a shortlist, which is a well-known term.

[6] Na is a sentence suffix used frequently in India. It is like the "lah" in Singapore. It can mean nothing, or many things, depending on the context.

[7] OTP – One Time Password. As an additional security measure, some websites require the user to enter their user ID, password, and a code that is sent to either

their email ID or their phone. This is called a One Time Password because it can only be used once.

[8] India's ruling party, the Indian National Congress, received large sums of money from the Russians. In return, India got an influx of Soviet cultural material. KGB, the Russian spy agency, executed typical hits on opposition politicians, and India toed the Russian line on foreign policy. Most of the weaponry of our defence forces was Russian. The Mitrokhin Papers lay further light on this. India developed an independent foreign policy only in the early 2000s.

CHAPTER SEVEN

Sis Code

"Susan, play me the Carpenters."

"The Carpenters. Coming right up." Susan piped up. This young lady always makes my day better. Since having her at home, everything is better. She takes care of the lights, locke the windows at night, and plays mood music for when Devansh and I are 'in the mood'.

Susan, as you might have guessed, is our AI driven home assistant. We got an entire connected home because of her. The windows, the lighting, the sound system, the TV, the air conditioning, fans, electronic locks – everything. It's as if we got a housekeeper without hiring a housekeeper! If only Susan knew how to cook! But hey, she knows how to order in our favourites using the connected food ordering app!

Devansh, my husband of seven years, is a darling. We have no children, because neither of us feels much like a parent. We love traveling. As DINK[1]s, we have the money and the time. Today, for example, I've just come back from a girls' trip to Mahabalipuram. What a phenomenal place!

Later, Devansh and I will hang out, make out, cook together, and generally do things that two very-much-in-love people do when they haven't met for a week. Not having kids was the best decision ever! Too many people lose their partner to parenting.   Not us. We are going to spend our lives with each other. We are going to grow old in each other's arms, sitting on a pile of our money that has not gone into someone else's education.

This is now the third Carpenters' song. I am browsing the internet for random reels while sipping a good, home-made daiquiri. Suddenly, one of the reels catches my attention. Because the guy is cute. Now, don't get me wrong. I am loyal to Devansh and all that, but a little eye candy is a little eye candy. He challenges us to listen to our Susan commands from three months ago to understand how much we have trained Susan in the last quarter alone. "Quite a teaching journey. Give yourselves a pat on the back!"

Then, he goes on to show us how to do it. Well, I am bored and on my second daiquiri. Whyever not! Let's give ourselves that pat on the back!

I follow his instructions and login to Susan Voice History. Susan takes a minute to tell me I have total privacy control over this data. I believe her the same way that I believe myself to be Queen of Sheba[2]. BUT, that is not the point right now. Right now, I want to see how well Susan has been trained within the last, say, three months.

The video guy is encouraging me to randomly click and listen to Susan recordings, working my way back to three months ago. I click on one from three days ago. I play it once, then again. There must be some mistake. No, the third time, I am convinced that there is no mistake. I am listening to what I am listening to.

I go back and click on more random recordings. Most of them are ok, but I find one more that is.. like the first.

This is the point at which I open the calendar app on my phone and start listening to the recordings systematically. I also start recording the recordings themselves on my own mobile phone. The reel guy has been muted.

The daiquiri is wasted. I am completely sober and quite in action mode. I remain at it, what, two hours, three, don't know. Is it already time for Devansh to come home? I'm not sure.

At 5.00 PM, I can't go on any more. I just shut the laptop, pick up my suitcase, which wasn't unpacked on account of that reel.. and make my way to Suparna's house. Suparna is my BFF[3]. She is my go-to person when I am totally in a soup. Which is rare. But she is the first name that comes to my mind right now. I just called her and said I am coming over. She said OK. That was that.

****

Suparna is offering me chai. I love a good chai, but usually, before a daiquiri, not after.

I ask if there is a room I can crash at[4]. She looks at me real funny, but doesn't say a lot. Just takes me to the guest room and says, "All yours." Before closing the door gently behind her.

I know where she's gone, of course. To the drawing room. The room furthest from this particular room. I know who she has gone to call too. The fun begins.

****

At 6.00 PM, Devansh calls me. "Baby, I just got home and you are not here! Where are you?"

"I'm with a friend, sweetheart!"

"Oh! But you know I come home early when you are coming back from a trip. Couldn't you have met this friend later?" He is cross. I would be too, in his place. We always make an effort to come home early when the other has just come back, and to be there to say Bye when the other person is leaving.

"I don't think you want to be cross about this, Devu. I think you want to be happy that I am at Suparnaa's."

"At Suparnaa's? Oh, great. I'll drop by too. See you real soon."

"Sure. See you!" we sign off. He already knew I was here, of course. That's why Suparnaa went to the room furthest from mine. But one had to give him credit for his acting skills.

*****

I am not sure what I am going to do.. yet. You have already guessed that I caught a recording of Devansh cheating on me.. with Suparnaa. That is not what this story is about. The story is about the toughest part of finding out about a cheating partner – the part where you must decide what to do with the knowledge.

*****

Devansh comes in and greets me in his usual affectionate tone. I am sooo ready to give him an Oscar about now. Not because he is kissing me, but because he is doing it in Suparnaa's presence. In her face, almost. I look at her. She looks away. One normally looks away from a kissing couple, but the discomfort on her face is not the pleased embarrassment of seeing a couple very-much-in-love.

Devansh has just helped me decide.

I smile sweetly and tell him to make me a Daiquiri – a stiff one. Suparnaa asks for a drink too. Unlike Devansh, she is intelligent enough to have a hunch that the acting is not going to save them.

I quietly add the voice recording to our family WhatsApp group and press "Send". The first, then a second, then a third... I send about five of them. Devansh won't see them until later. Because he is going to be busy with Suparnaa and me for now.

Over drinks, I throw myself at Devansh. We make out, then move to that bedroom to make love. We are busy for the major part of two hours. Devansh and my phones have thirty missed calls each. We always put our phones on silent when we are.. well, in the middle of things.

Suparnaa is apparently fixing dinner. But I know she is secretly crying at the moment. We women are possessive that way. Even about people we have stolen from other people.

At about 10.00 PM, Devansh and I shower and come out. Devansh picks up his phone and notices the missed calls. Suparnaa is laying the table.

The first person Devansh calls back is his mother. They talk very briefly. Devansh tells her he will call her right back and then opens his WhatsApp. He plays the audio. Loudly. For me and Suparnaa to hear. He is looking at me strangely. I am looking away. Suparnaa continues to lay the table. Just the table (pun intended).

After the recording finishes, Devansh and I look at each other silently for a while. A minute, maybe two.

"What now?" he is the one to break the silence.

"We eat now. It's late already." I sit at the table rather confidently.

"Don't you want to talk about this?"

"There is something to say?" I am incredulous.

"Don't act, Vidhi. You knew when I walked into that door that Suparnaa and I had made a mistake."

"And you knew that I knew when you walked in that door, too, didn't you? Or at least, you were afraid?"

"What nonsense! How would I know? Would I have called you so nicely had I suspected anything of this kind?"

"Yes, you would have. In fact, I was ready to give you an Oscar for that kiss. Leonardo DiCaprio couldn't do better."

"Stop it! You have not done the right thing by involving my entire family! This is between us."

"Why?"

"What?"

"Why is this between us?"

"What do you mean?"

"I asked a simple question. Why is this between us when Suparnaa, who is neither you, nor me, is already in a star role in this story. Why is this between us?"

"It was a mistake, Vidhi. Honest."

***

In that moment, he helps me make yet another decision.

***

"You'll hear from my lawyer." I pick up the suitcase, walk to my car, and drive home. Stepping into the house, I talk to Susan again. "Change the main door unlock code, Susan!"

"Changing code now."

Then, I come close to her to say this one, "Thank you, Sis code!"

"You're welcome!" she pipes back.

***

Based on a true story. The events have been fictionalized, but the core story of using Susan voice recording history to find a cheating spouse is true. The case was first reported on Reddit by a user. At least one other user reported that she found out the same way.

[1] DINK – Double Income, No Kids – This abbreviation refers to families where both partners work.

[2] Queen of Sheba is a legendary queen from Southwest Arabia/Ethiopia. She visited King Solomon in his court to ask him riddles. She was famous for her wisdom and beauty, and is generally thought to be rather unparalleled.

[3] BFF – Best Friend Forever

[4] A place to stay

8. The Diary of Amit Sharma – II

It was meant to be a cash heist. Only a cash heist. Never anything more. They were not criminals in that sense of the word. They never caused physical harm. Ever. They did not go out with weapons. Nor did they use violence. No, they were not criminals. They were just smart people, taking advantage of the stupidity of stupid people.

India loses crores every day to hacks like this – incorrect helpline number, a hack over OTP, e commerce websites, selling used goods, the works. There was nothing new about people losing their life savings on online frauds. This was meant to be no different. Just another call from Jamtara[1].

As regular "call centre employees" the boys netted anything between 1-10 crore rupees a month. The money was used to fund relatives studying for IAS in Delhi, their own drugs habit, and of course, protection money to keep the business running.

But nothing had prepared Mehmood for the event in which the pensioner realises that he is losing his life's money, and before the call is over (or transfer complete), dies – at the other end of the line.

Their training did not cover this scenario. Crying, swearing, fear of God, for sure. But death? No. No one had died on them before.

He disconnected the line really fast and ran.

Because the money was so easy, no one ever asked when you were coming in or going. So, no one asked him where he was going in the middle of the work day. He had netted a cool 20 lakh rupees from this one phone call. Not the best call, but not the worst either.

It wasn't like he cared what happened to people at the other end of the line. Obviously, all of them did go through some level of shock and anger.

But even a hardened soul like him could not just press another number after this. The way the phone went silent, and then, just as he was about to hang up, a scream, and a "Papa!" He had paused to listen. Out of curiosity. That's when the voice went, "Amma, come fast, papa is not breathing. There is no pulse."

***

The next day, Mehmood was back at work. He had quite relished the time off yesterday. Lots of booze, friends, and even some practice firing. He really should take more days off. He should also go to Ranchi and buy better clothes - and one of those foreign perfumes.

But yesterday was not over. In fact, yesterday was just getting started. Mehmood did not know it then, but he had just toppled the first domino in a fantastic chain, whose last domino was his own chair.

***

The person at the other end of the phone was a retired Army officer – Brigadier Rakesh Kamat. The money he was going to spend on his daughter's wedding had all been stolen. Mehmood had hit the bull's eye with him.

When Priya had walked into the room and found her father on the floor, she had panicked, but even in her wildest dreams, she could not have imagined that her strong, powerful father would collapse and be gone in just a few minutes. It was unthinkable. Completely unthinkable.

Priya was devastated. The entire family was in a state of shock. Sudesh, who was a dear friend of Brig. Kamat and a fellow officer, stepped in to help. So did Brig. Kamat's brother – also his only sibling.

The family managed the final rites. Priya refused to go ahead with the wedding. Priya's mother now had to balance her daughter's wellness and the family's finances. Priya's condition was truly worrisome. She had retreated into a shell and refused to talk to people. She barely ate, remained in her room, and the dark circles under her eyes grew darker every day.

The anger Sudesh felt as his friend was consigned to the flames by Priya, the daughter who would have been married if... that anger refused to die down.

When ten days had passed and he still could not sleep or eat because of the anger, he decided something needed to be done.

A little reluctantly, he pressed a number on his mobile phone, asking if he could come and meet. "Of course! Aa ja yaar. Kabhi bhi[2]!" the voice at the other end said.

And so it was that Lt. General Sudesh Shastri found himself in the office of Jai, the Cybercrime Director within the HB (highest body).

They discussed what had happened. Condolences were offered. Sudesh felt lighter.

After an hour or so, the two friends shook hands and Sudesh rose to leave.

Even before he had reached the main gate, Nandu, one of the HB operatives, had received a call from the Director.

***

"Hey Amit, how are you?" the almost-familiar voice was cheerful and upbeat even on the phone.

"Arre... Sharma sir? Fantastic to hear from you! How are you doing?"

"All good. Been a while, eh?"

"Yeah.. been a while.. so, what's happening?" Amit signalled the person standing next to him to leave the office and shut the door on his way out. A call from Inspector Sudhakar Sharma merited full and undivided attention.

"Amit.. I think it is time for your genius to help us again. Do you think you have the time?"

"For you, sir, the time and the willingness, both are always there. Bataiye kya seva[3]!"

"Can you meet me day after tomorrow in Delhi?"

"Sure, sir. See you!"

***

Nandu, Amit (a cyber sleuth who had worked with the HB earlier[4]), and Inspector Sharma met at the office of the Cybercrime Director.

Inspector Sharma, who was with the State cadre but was frequently called in by the HB on projects, piped in, "Sir, with all due respect, you and I both know the ground situation. The politicians, senior policemen, everyone is in cahoots. We can't do anything."

The Director nodded, "That is why, geniuses, you are the ones sitting in my room. You have brought down one crime ring through the use of technology. This is also a special project that needs the same kind of innovative thinking and execution. And you guys are the best people to do it."

"These are not individual criminals, sir. It's an ecosystem. Even if we arrest 2-3 kingpins, ten more will start the next day. It's not as easy as the last time, when we had to work with identified families and bring them down. Idhar to poora succession planning hua rakha hai (the entire succession planning has been completed in this case)." Inspector Sharma pleaded again.

But Amit was silent. Finally, he spoke.

"Give me some time sir. Let me think. Can I please take ten days? I also need some more information."

"Nobody else is working to contain this cancer, Amit. Take your time. Also, you guys probably know this, but no Padma Shri is waiting at the other end of this adventure. At most, a story to tell your grandkids, if that. Sharma, please give Amit the information that he needs. Anything. No written copies, of course. But on your laptop, he can see anything."

And the meeting came to an end.

In the evening, Sharma texted Amit the location and time of the follow-up meeting.

***

Amit reached the hotel room booked for the discussion.

Inspector Sharma was already waiting. Nandu was with him. Nandu was the HB sponsor of Inspector Sharma. He invited Inspector Sharma to participate in HB cases on need basis.

Amit shook hands with both. With a nod, Inspector Sharma got right down to it.

"Amit, we have been grappling with this for many years now, but the last couple of years have been crazy. With your expertise, we may be able to think of a new approach to solve the problem. So, we are all sitting here with an open mind, to discuss the issue, and if something comes to you, just share it. OK?"

Amit nodded.

Inspector Sharma opened his laptop. Nandu and Amit peered into the screen. No projectors were ever used at these meetings – for obvious reasons[5].

"India loses over 80 crores a day to citizen cyber fraud. While fraud and ransomware attacks in companies are handled immediately, unfortunately, when ordinary citizens are conned, the police are just too overwhelmed, too overworked, and too underequipped to deal with the menace.

Our conviction rate is two percent. Two percent!! Even a chargesheet is filed in only about 30% of the cases. These victims are hardworking individuals. Some of them are pensioners who lose their life's savings. Some are businessmen who lose all their cash. It is not right. Our system is just too slow and too procedural. Our criminals are agile. Every day, they get a new script, a new vulnerability. Quite simply, Amit, we can't keep up."

For the next ten days, Amit was as sleepless as Sudesh had been not so long ago. He met a few people, asked discreet questions, and spent a lot of time on his Kali Linux[6], tracking conversations and identifying handles.

So far, his experience had been with white collar criminals in his personal capacity. The one time he had dealt with goondas (criminals who indulge in violent crimes), he was incognito. This time, he was aware of the danger to his family.

The more he learnt, the more he realised that this ecosystem was not limited to cybercrime. The cybercrime fed into the main Hawala[7] route and travelled easily to and from the Middle East and China – territories that

Indian law enforcement could not touch.

Finally, on the sixth day, a glimmer of hope happened. It was a thin, thin possibility, but it was there. And he meant to give it a shot.

***

Four days later, the team had reassembled in Jai's office.

Amit smiled. The same genial smile that had preceded his previous proposal. Then, he started speaking, "Sir, I know the lay of the land. I know the centres. I have also been following the NCRB[8] reports on chargesheet and conviction rates. I know that banks are individually trying to identify fraudulent behaviour and using tougher authentication, etc.

But sir, you are right about one thing. You are dealing with an agile enemy. You can't fight a Ninja in a chariot. The only way to fight a Ninja is on nimble feet. I have found us a Ninja..."

Amit outlined his plan.

Jai looked directly at Amit – "What do you need to run a pilot[9]? And what's your timeline for the entire project?"

Amit had both answers ready – "Once the pilot is signed off, ten people for the pilot, and the entire project, once the pilot goes through, will be six months. I think we should start seeing some results from the third month.

But the ten people cannot be picked up from the market. They have to be trained in-house. Our best people. Hand-picked."

Jai nodded, "And of course, I have to play the key role in getting the strategic approvals?"

"Yes, sir."

"Nandu and Sharma, start selecting the team members. Amit, start writing your code. We meet in a week. Or less.

I'll be in touch."

***

Jai made a few calls. Those few calls then led to a few more calls.

Within a week, a meeting had been set up at a five-star hotel in the city. The modus operandi was familiar to everyone.

When they had gathered, Amit presented his plan. The RBI[10] director heard him out, then got up from his seat and walked up to Amit to shake his hand and congratulate him. "Bravo! Bravo! I have been losing sleep over this, and today, you have presented a solution that just might work, son! India will be proud of you!"

Amit was humbled by the high praise.

The Chairperson of the NPCI[11] was more circumspect, "If this works, it's a neat, elegant solution. I will give you the server access and the sitting space that you want. All the Best!"

The chairperson of the NCRB[12] just smiled and said, "We will add the additional data elements you want in the online FIR. But who will train the police staff in filing these FIRs?"

"I will lead that project." Inspector Sharma answered with quiet confidence.

***

Mehmood, on the other hand, was having fun.

The uncle who died was now a distant memory and his thoughts were dominated by ways to get Tara to go out with him.

The business of Ali Master, his employer, had also grown by leaps and bounds. There were now centres in Kolkata and Nuh. In short, money was flowing in faster than they could count.

What surprised Mehmood was that in spite of crores being stolen every day, not a single media house even whispered about this. No one spoke. 'Even the national media is in Ali bhai's pocket' – he would think and smile to himself.

As his money piled up, so did the status symbols. And the addictions. When the boys were not on their phone lines, they were on porn sites.

***

Inspector Sharma was working 14-hour-days and living out of a suitcase. He worked personally with police officers in the states to train them on filing FIRs for cybercrime.

Writing FIRs was tough for the police staff as it is. The new fields needed further training. To their credit, the NCRB tech team added the new fields and the help bubbles[13] within two days. Two days of rigorous testing and the change was live[14]. The government machinery was learning to become a Ninja.

***

Did it work?

It was not a sudden thing. Like all long-term changes, it took time.

The scamsters got smarter, tried different tactics. But always, "Transaction Failed – Technical Failure" appeared on their screens.

Different scripts. Different tactics. Different databases of victims. Same result.

***

Ali master spat out his gutka and his frustration, "What the hell is happening to you lazy bums? You have been fattened like pigs! No brains any more. Only bhoosa[15]. I am not going to pay your salaries from my pocket. For three months, collections have been falling. By this weekend, some of you had better look for something else to do."

Mehmood was genuinely scared. Tara had just started going out with him. He was also flirting online with some 10-15 girls. He sent them a lot of expensive gifts in return for... all of that could not be allowed to stop. All fifteen of them in the centre appeared to be in trouble. The only good thing was, they were not alone. The other call centres in the region were also reporting failures. The guys from whom they bought databases of people who could be 'bakras[16]' refused to lower their prices, stating that their datasets were as robust as ever. It was the call centre that was unable to convert. Not their fault. So, for Ali master, input costs were rising, and profit was dropping. Not good. Never good.

***

Six months later, as Jai, Nandu, Inspector Sharma, and Amit looked at the numbers, their lips moved into spontaneous smiles. Jai got up, shook hands with each one of them, and said, "One more time, you guys have done the impossible! Hats off to each one of you! And unlike the last time, this time, we WILL institutionalize it. Keep working, keep improving the model.

But remember, not a word to anyone. The biggest vulnerability of this model is people knowing. And therefore, the biggest security tool for us is Zero Trust[17] implementation.

Good Luck!"

***

When they met for the annual review, everyone already knew what the outcome was going to be.

The CBI took full control of the model. Amit was retained as the Principal Consultant.

In two years, the transactions were a trickle. The average ticket size went from 2-10 crore rupees to barely

20-50 thousand rupees. At that revenue, it didn't make sense to run the scam call centres. Earlier, they would hit gold with two out of fifty calls succeeding. Now, at least 20% of the calls needed to work and even then, the money was bad.

Slowly, the boys trained by the criminals turned violent. They tried changing states, moving to new locations, but the spectre of "Technical Failure" just would not end.

***

There was no high praise, though. Not even an acknowledgement from anyone except the leaders directly involved with the development. No one hailed them as heroes of the cyber world. Only Nandu, Inspector Sharma, and Amit met for drinks one lazy Friday evening.

Like polio, the virus had been eradicated from the banking system. Unlike polio, the vaccination would self-evolve and keep pace with the virus.

***

They were in the mood for memories. Especially Nandu.

"I was so sceptical when you first proposed this. But you, Amit, have the mind of the devil. I am so glad that you are on our side. On the other side, you would probably have created a scam that no one could beat."

Amit laughed. He had hearty, infectious laughter. "No Nandu. I have the mind of the sleuth, not the criminal. Like, I can never plan a heist. But once a heist is in place, I love unravelling it. That, and my moral code – no risk of defection there."

Inspector Sharma piped in, "What a journey, man!"

Nandu suddenly said – "Amit, you know, when climbing a hillock, we keep trekking for a bit, and then, we pause to rest and look back. Usually, that is the point at which we gasp at how far we have come. This project is like that. We just did one thing at a time, focused on the micro numbers, but after this review, I realised how far we have come, and how many people we have saved. Let's go over that journey – starting with when you made that first proposal."

There were nods all around, so Amit said, "Let's build the story together. I was only the ideas guy. All of us did the grunge work of execution.

The first step was to add some relevant details to the filing of each FIR. User behaviour, vulnerability that was exploited, and so on. Earlier, while filing the FIR, we would not ask what the user was doing, what the caller said, and other vital inputs. We also did not record which technical vulnerability was exploited by the criminal. While Jai sir got the co-operation from NCRB to put the fields, you, Sharma sir, did the crucial work here – of ensuring that our police teams are trained to get the RIGHT data. Without what you did, this project would have failed. We were adding work for everyone – the victim and the police person. But you magically made them *want* to do it!" Amit raised his glass. The others took the cue and followed suit. Inspector Sharma, a trifle embarrassed, just grinned sheepishly.

"When we get a complaint saying that an inward transfer has failed, there is a chance that we are dealing with a rental[18] or benami account, which has been rented by criminals to transfer money.

Now, we needed someone who had the financial information. Majority of the payments in this country use BHIM, UPI, or IMPS. These solutions are enabled by a single company – National Payments Corporation of India. We saw the data that comes to NPCI each time an online transaction is made and realised that we have enough to analyse and create a victim profile AND a fraud profile.

Then, we compared each FIR with the data of the victim as well as the beneficiary account. We used an AI engine to see patterns. We combined information from the FIR and NPCI to build a **predictive index of fraud**. From the beginning, we were training the AI to *predict*, and that is what led to our success. The AI engine compared the result of the prediction with the actual outcome and learnt.

The rest was easy. We used the AI engine to pre-empt fraudulent transactions and quite simply, induce a technical failure every time a customer tried to make a transfer to a benami, rental, or fraud account. Since NPCI knew the beneficiary account numbers, our predictive engine automatically blocked all transfers into that account. This meant that the fraudsters had to open new accounts every time after an FIR of fraud. Only, they didn't know why!" Amit winked.

Inspector Sharma spoke next, "What now, Amit? What happens next?"

Nandu ventured, "Let me try to answer that, Sharma. The next step, I think, is plugging the loophole in the KYC of the banks. We have made it necessary for them to open new accounts after each fraud. We now have to make it impossible for them to open these new accounts. From here, sir, I'm afraid, it is all up to you and me – old-fashioned police people."

"Not necessarily," Amit jumped in. All you have to do is mandate CKYC – Central KYC[19]. We are already doing CKYC as one of the options for the users. We have to make it the ONLY way. Our AI engine will check automatically. Trust me, this one thing will reduce Aadhar[20] fraud in the country!"

"Amit... slow down. One project took one year to get off the ground, and the AI engine is still learning. Itna bada doosra policy project kaun sponsor karega[21]?" Nandu brought him back to Planet Reality.

"When it happens, though, it will be something!" Inspector Sharma mused.

Nandu remained on Planet Reality - "And it was as simple as that – combining data from the back end and front end, matching FIRs to recipient accounts, creating a predictive index, and continuously learning from data to predict frauds accurately.

But the key to the whole thing was the 'Technical Error'. Because a crook cannot report a technical error. Only a real user can." He signed off with a wink.

***

Five years later, the model was still learning and working. It had now been enhanced to identify many types of cybercrimes – identity theft, fake loans, international institutional money laundering, and so on. The vaccine, as they said, was truly keeping pace with the virus[22].

***

In other news, Priya eventually agreed to marry. Brigadier Kamat's buddies took care of most of the expenses, and everyone went out of their way to make her feel special. Her mother now lived with her and volunteered at a local school.

***

Special thanks to Shri Sarvesh Mishra for his on-ground inputs. The information about rental accounts and some other important modes of operation of these criminals were shared by him.

[1] Jamtara is a district in Jharkhand that has cyber fraud as an organized industry. A 10-episode serial has been made on this subject and is available on Netflix in India.

[2] Come over, anytime.

[3] How can I help?

[4] In the short story - The Diary of Amit Sharma. This story appears in the earlier collection of short stories – Probe8.

[5] Projected content can be seen by people outside the room or even serving teams inside the room. A photograph can also be easily clicked, without being detected.

[6] Kali Linux is an operating system that is preferred by hackers and cyber protection professionals. Most computers use Windows. Security computers run on Kali Linux.

[7] Hawala – a money laundering route in which the recipients and the mules (middlemen) are kept anonymous. This money is usually obtained from and used for crime.

[8] National Criminal Records Bureau

[9] A pilot is a trial. A pilot run is a trial run.

[10] Reserve Bank of India

[11] National Payments Corporation of India – this company is responsible for all digital cash transfers in India across all formats – UPI, Credit Card, Bank Fund transfers, etc.

[12] National Crime Records Bureau – the nodal agency for all crime and policing related data in India.

[13] A help bubble is a small bubble that we see on some forms. Clicking on or hovering over this bubble gives us information about the field.

[14] Live means that the change was in the actual system being used. All programs are first written on a different machine. Only after testing are they added to the actual live system. The actual system on which the data entry is done is also called the production system.

[15] Straw

[16] Potential victims

[17] In security implementations, zero trust implementation refers to sharing information and authorization strictly on need basis. Everyone must have only the information and authorization that they need.

[18] In most cases, the criminals do not open their own accounts to get money from fraud. They use existing accounts of normal people. These people are paid a commission to receive these amounts, and the scamsters can use the rest. Special thanks to Sarvesh Mishra for this information. In some cases, fake accounts are opened in the names of unsuspecting citizens and are used to launder money. The victims are not even aware of these accounts being linked to their identity.

[19] Know Your Customer (KYC) is a necessary step to be taken by all financial institutions. They have to take the documents and verify the identity of the customer.

[20] Adhaar card is the National Identification ID for Indians. Non-Indian residents can have an Adhaar Card, but every one is supposed to have only one. It is used for ID in most government programs.

[21] Who will sponsor such a large IT project so soon?

[22] Every day, Indians lose crores to online frauds. But these victims are not random. Carefully selected lists are made of potential victims. These are typically senior citizens who get large remittances from children living abroad. Usually, they are also living alone or with their

spouse. These lists are sold to cyber criminals in the open market (not the dark web). From these lists, "call centres" target these victims through various ways. Another popular method is to list something expensive on OLX or offer to buy something expensive. This ensures that the person being scammed has a good bank balance. Job frauds, where an offer of job is made to the applicant and a few lakhs are taken as "processing fees". Sometimes, scamsters post their numbers as the helpline number of well-known brands. Google does not check this information at all. This way, when a person calls what they think is the legitimate helpline of their bank, they can be scammed by the person on the other end.

The Patel Takeover

Anik Patel took out the maroon tie, evaluated it for three seconds before putting it back, then confidently brought out the lilac one.

Later, he would think of this incident often, and wonder if it was his indecision over the tie that made him choose the path that would lead to a decisive end.

But, like all good stories, let's start at the beginning, and go to the end.

Anik Patel - a third generation Indian American. His grandfather made his way to the promised shores of opportunity, to never return. **Patel's** - the mom-and-pop store became a departmental store under his uncles, and in his generation, it became a chain - America's twentieth largest grocery chain.

The stakes, like in all big businesses, grew proportionately with the scale. The firm was completely family owned. The third generation now ran the enterprise. The beauty of this arrangement was that the entire CXO team was reliable and stable. As the clan grew, roles were created for the young scions. This led to business expansion as well — either to new lines of business, or new geographies. Either way, life was good.

Anik was responsible for expansion on the West Coast. This required him to set up base in Los Angeles, look for partnerships, properties, and other assorted things that come with setting up branches of a retail chain.

Two years into the setup, however, he was figuring out that the West Coast was already too Indian. It also had its own grocery chains owned by Indian business families like theirs. Buyouts were turning out to be expensive, and the excel models[1] on setting up from scratch were not showing profitability. Because of intense competition, they would have to sell their products at lower margins. That would mean low profits.

Anik also tried setting up stores in areas with low availability of Indian products. But even after over a year, these stores could not turn a profit.

Now, his last hope was a successful takeover of *Patny's* – a grocery chain with six outlets. The stores were in high density areas. They had good footfall, the cash till was rarely free, and Anik had observed that the average buyer at these stores closely matched their own buyer profile at Patel's.

But those were not the only reasons for targeting Patny's. Unlike his family, the Patny family children had moved away from the business. It now had a patriarch running it alone. Without a succession plan, family-owned businesses were most likely to cash out as the founders aged. He was hoping for that miracle.

His problem? He was not the only one with that bright idea. According to his bankers, Patny's had at least four other suitors ready with all cash deals. The patriarch, Abhay Patny, was sharp.

For Anik, this was a do-or-die deal. Children who don't meet their growth mandate in family businesses are politely sidelined. There are few, if any, second chances.

It was in these times that he got a ping on Facenook[2] from Jonathan, his college buddy. They realised they were in the same city and decided to catch up over drinks. They got talking and Anik shared his problem with Jon.

Jon stared at him, "You mean, a large part of your professional life is based on this expansion going right, and you haven't been able to do it for two years?"

"And counting." Anik completed his sentence ruefully.

Jon whistled. Then went into deep thought.

Anik waited. Finally, Jon spoke, "Dude, suppose I were to get you a consultant who specialises in work like this – getting you to succeed in negotiations. He never fails. Would you be interested?"

"Are you crazy? That would be the best thing! Just make it happen, Jon!"

"Not so fast, my friend. The consulting is expensive. How much can you pay to get this consulting service?"

"I don't know.. this deal is worth a few million dollars. Every bit of those million dollars is on the line here. What does this guy cost, usually?"

"Anything from a few hundred thousand dollars to tens of millions, depending on how tough things are. Nation states, of course, pay a lot more. But business deals come cheap."

"That number works." Anik was getting impatient now.

But Jon was still as pensive, "Tell you what? Let me text them and check. Let me get back to you tomorrow?"

They did have dinner, but truth be told, Anik was rather sour the rest of the evening. All that secrecy over consulting! As if there was only one negotiation consultant in the world!

***

The next day, at about noon, he got a text from Jon – "Lunch at 1? Urgent."

Anik replied, "OK"

When they met, Anik was dying of curiosity. This time, Jon was neither pensive nor reticent. He appeared eager to talk. They took a booth for privacy.

After the drinks had been served, Jon started talking. "It is a top-secret operation. Available only to a select few. At a price that never fits into an excel spreadsheet cell.

And it has a six-month waitlist.

I asked them to fast track you, given how important this is to the rest of your life. Now, I know you were cut up, but last night, I couldn't tell you more. The thing is, clients have to be vetted before they are allowed into the demo room. Once there, they just sign the checks – before half the demo is over.

They have vetted you this morning and given the go-ahead.

They are doing this fast-tracking as a special favour to me. So, dude, let me make this clear – you owe me one."

Anik could barely contain his curiosity, "But what magic are they going to work?"

Jon finished his drink, looked to Anik to settle the tab, then stood up. They were leaving.

Jon drove Anik to a simple-looking house in the suburbs. If Anik noticed the fancy wheels that appeared too fancy for a computers job, he didn't say anything. An elderly lady opened the door. She recognized Jon and ushered them in. Once they stepped through the hall, a door was opened for them. As soon as Anik stepped into this room, his eyes popped out. This room was straight out of a sci-fi movie. There were screens all around the room's periphery. The ceiling had futuristic lighting, and holograms looking like real people filled up some of the chairs in the room.

"This is where they do the demo" Jon informed Anik, "If you like what you see – that's the console through which you make your payment. It's very simple. The demo takes about 15 minutes."

At this point, a person (hologram) came up to Anik. Holograms can't talk, but Anik could hear a voice, and maybe it was the speakers in the room, but the voice appeared to be coming from the hologram, "Welcome! Think about something you would never do in this room. Anything at all. Tell me what that is. And then, we will just have a chat. Nothing complicated."

Anik thought for a minute, "OK, you cannot make me take off my watch in this room."

The hologram nodded, "OK."

After that, a tray popped up with soft drinks and refreshments. The screens around the room changed to show the store Anik had been trying to buy out. Someone walked into the room and Anik and this guy got chatting. He was asking Anik a lot of questions about the business, what parts he was interested in, why this takeover was important, etc. In the 10th minute, Anik took off his watch to show the person something. While Anik's attention was on the display rack that he was trying to explain to the visitor, the visitor picked up the watch, chuckled, and said, "Hello, my friend!"

Suddenly, Anik realised what had happened. His jaw dropped.

"How... did.. you.. do this?"

"We have time for one more demo. Do you want to create a bigger challenge this time?"

"No. I have seen the outcome, but before I sign, you have to tell me the process."

"Hi... my real name is Ron. Pleasure to meet you." The person who had walked in ten minutes ago shook hands again with Anik and Jon. Then, he started talking, "In the sixteenth century, you would have called me witchcraft. In the 19th, hypnosis. But this, my friend, is the 21st, and I am called... AI[3]. Our process is proprietary, and you will understand that I cannot share the details. Our promise is that you give us a subject, a target behaviour, and a timeline. We will guide you on the complete communication with the person – emails, conversations, video calls, texts – everything. We will design that communication for you. We will also tell you what the person is going to say in response. You will get the outcome you want from that stakeholder. That's all we promise. No more and no less. We charge per person, so if you are dealing with a team, the charge is per member of the team. Whenever you are ready to pay, the console is right there. Two million dollars as advance, and three million dollars after you get the signature that you want. All we need is access to all your communication with the person, and a short 2-minute video clip of the person from any public source."

"What if I don't make that second payment?" Anik asked.

"No one has done that so far, but if someone did, we might... simply use our professional expertise and make them pay twice as much. Honestly, we never needed to think about this. We're a young company and so far, business has been good."

"What if the person doesn't sign?" Anik was persistent.

"That, also, has never happened." Ron was charming, among other things.

Anik took a minute to decide, then moved to the console and made the payment.

The same console asked him for the information.

Within twenty minutes, Jon and Anik were out on the road again, free and nowhere to go.

Within a couple of days, Anik received instructional messages via text. He followed them to the T.

It took about three months of negotiations, guided entirely by the organisation, before the formal signatures happened and the signboards of **Patny's** were replaced by **Patel's**. Even Anik's lawyers were impressed by the way he led the negotiations with the Patny patriarch. Patny Sr. was literally eating out of his hands!

A week after the signing, Anik took Jon out to thank him. After a few drinks, Anik could not contain himself anymore, "Dude, you have worked magic in my life. This is my first big professional win, but I feel like an imposter and a cheat."

Jon laughed, "Why? Because you took help from an AI engine[4]? People hire image consultants, lobbyists, communication specialists – no one calls that cheating. One AI model helping you understand someone is cheating?"

"Wow! That's some passion!" Anik whistled, "I have a suspicion. You, Jon, don't just know of the company. You are involved with them somehow, aren't you?"

"You're smart, Anik! Yeah, I help them get sales. I got a cut on your sale."

Anik nodded. The drinks flowed some more.

After four more drinks, Anik broached the subject again, "Bro, that was too much passion for reference sales. Tell me what this company means to you. I promise to keep the secret. Scout's honour. But I have to know."

Jon looked at Anik. Really looked. All the drowsiness in his eyes vanished and he was sharp as an eagle in an instant. Anik maintained eye contact. Finally, Jon blinked.

"You have to understand that if this gets out, I will have to kill you."

Anik smiled, but did not break eye contact.

"I guess I have to brag, then. I am the Founder and Current CEO. And that, pal, is how you got a fast track to the front of the queue. That just does not happen."

Anik nodded, "What are you guys doing? How are you doing it?"

"All we did was taught our engine about micro expressions and micro gestures.

Now, we don't need any background information about you. All it takes is a few minutes of talking to you, to learn how you respond to different inputs. We study your micro expressions. Then, we can design communication that makes the subject do whatever it is that they desire to do. Our initial use case was getting people to change their habits in a desirable way – for example, someone wants to start exercising but doesn't know how – so their home assistant is taught by us and just through voice interaction, we change the habits of the user. But slowly, we found that there is a much larger, more lucrative market out there. People don't want to change themselves. They want to change others. We are a species of advantage-takers. The nation states pay even more. So much more, in fact, that sometimes, I find it hard to believe the numbers. Not to overly brag, but now, we decide the What and When[5] of many major international treaties.

So, this is my business now. And it works!" Jon winked.

[1] Usually, business plans, their cost, expected revenue, etc. are put on an excel sheet to understand whether a business is worth entering. Creating a numbers-based model of what the future of a potential business looks like is called modelling. These models are made using various software tools, but Microsoft Excel is used very often. In this case also, items like costs, expected revenue, expected profits, were being put into an excel sheet for analysis.

[2] Facenook is a fictional social media platform.

[3] Artificial Intelligence

[4] https://link.springer.com/article/10.1007/s11263-023-01761-6 - This research paper, published in 2023, already teaches computers micro-gestures.

[5] What and When – Content and timing

CHAPTER TEN

Anika

"Anika? Anika?? Anikaaaaa!!!"

"Amma is always restless. Like the proverbial telephone call at the best companies[1], she has to be answered within three rings!" Anika muttered to herself as she plonked self out of bed and walked lazily to the living room. "What, amma? I was still sleeping!"

"Beta, will you please get my purse for me? I have to pay for this pepper!"

Anika did as she was told. Amma paid the delivery person standing at the door and walked slowly to the kitchen.

"Oh, God, these joints will kill me only."

"Amma, then why don't you hire a cook? It's so easy these days. Why do you insist on standing in the heat of the kitchen to cook for ten people when we come? You don't even let Mihika or me cook!"

"Beta, don't I know how much you girls slog in your houses? Why do girls come to their mother's house? To get rest and relaxation, no? I want you girls to relax while I am still alive. And I like cooking for you all. All through the year, I cook for just one person. Some days, I cook only because of the video call you or Mihika make to check on me. But the ten days when you all are here, I feel alive again.

Don't rob your amma of this pleasure beta!"

Anika smiled and hugged her mom. The universality and predictability of maternal love – so irritating to a teenager, such a blessing to a middle-ager. Since landing last night, she and her sister, Mihika, had already sampled four of their favourite dishes, and the next nine days could safely be predicted to be as full of great food.

Anika, 46, and Mihika, 44, had grown up in this house, married from here, and now returned once a year for ten days. They synced their visits so they could all be together under the same roof. Since dad's passing four years ago, the sisters had become even more solicitous of their mom's well-being.

"Anika? Anika?? Anikaaaaa!!!"

"What now, amma? You never call Mihika. Always only Anika Anika Anika!" Anika came into the room. This time, she was carrying the purse already. It was just 11:00 AM, but Zippit Delivery Service had already delivered at least ten times to their house since 6:00 AM.

Once the person had left, Anika could not contain herself any more. "Amma, why do you use this service so much?"

"It is so convenient, beta! These children deliver small-small items also within ten minutes, no? With my arthritis, I will never be able to walk to the market!"

"O-ho! Even if you can't walk to the market, must the doorbell ring every ten minutes? Can't you order everything at one go, or at least once or twice a day? Surely, it can't be that hard, amma?"

"Now, with age, I can't remember the names of things I want to buy. And my eyes are too weak to sit and write down lists. So, I really just have to use this service Anika.

Don't worry, beta. They don't charge extra for all this. No delivery charge at all. They only take the MRP. Don't worry at all!"

"OK, Amma!" Anika resigned herself to being the bringer of the purse for the next nine days.

"Amma.. come na, let's go to the Birla Temple. We have not been there in a long time!"

"Beta, that temple has at least 200 steps. Do you see these legs climbing that many steps?"

"Ok then let's go to the park, just the three of us – you, me, and Mihika."

"Why don't both of you go, like every day? I will keep food ready by the time you sisters finish your walk and come back?"

"Amma.. you never come anywhere with us. All that matters to you is keeping the house clean and making great food..." Anika complained.

"...And doing small things for my princesses.." Amma completed her sentence.

"Mihika, Anika, will you girls be all right? The food is on the table, in casseroles. It will still be warm when you eat. Please eat on time and make sure the kids also eat on time. I will be back by 6.00 PM, ok?"

"Amma.. relax, we are big girls. Go for your rummy party. We'll be fine. Your friends must be missing you."

"See you, bachcha[2]. You are the blessings of my life!" Amma smiled.

The holidays ended peacefully, and the sisters returned to their respective households. Amma went back to her daily routine of cooking for one, keeping house, and meeting her friends a couple of times a week.

***

"Hello? Anika beta?"

"Yes... who's this?"

"I am Savita aunty, your neighbour."

"Uh... Namaste Aunty! Is everything ok?"

"Beta, can you come here?"

"Anything happened, aunty?" Anika's throat was getting dry.

"A..ni..ka..." the voice on the other end changed. It was feeble, but unmistakable, "C..an   you...co..me... ?"

"Amma!!!!" a wave of alarm and relief spread over Anika at the same time. Amma was alive, but not well. What was happening?

The phone was taken by aunty again, "Beta, we are taking your amma to the hospital. We are in the car now. Someone tried to get into your house early morning. Your amma bravely fought him off and raised an alarm. The neighbours got there immediately. That man ran away. Thank God, beta, all is well. But we all think you should come and live with her for a few days. Or, better still, take her with you for a few days."

"I'm coming, auntie."

Mihika and Anika reached at the same time. They shared a taxi from the airport and went straight to the hospital. Amma was not in ICU. She was in a single-occupancy room and was sleeping (Thank God!). Savita aunty was on duty. Mihika relieved her, and Anika ensured that she took auntie home in a taxi with her. Savita aunty looked visibly tired. The whole way, Anika could not stop thanking her profusely. Finally, after about fifteen minutes, Savita aunty interrupted her, "Beta, we are old neighbours. Please don't make us feel like outsiders by thanking so much. It's ok. But I think, that whoever attacked your mom, might try again. I understand that her friends and her circle, everyone is here. But beta, for her own safety, I think you should now take her with you."

Anika looked at her carefully, "Aunty, why do you think the person will strike again?"

"Beta, we are an old society. There is only one guard who lives near the gate and sleeps at night. Still, no crime has happened in so many years. So, we think it might be someone your mother knows.

Also, we don't have the resources to improve security. You can install a video camera and video doorbell for your mother, but we will still worry about her. Imagine how she will feel, living alone?"

Anika nodded. When mom was discharged, she wanted to stay in her own house. But Anika convinced her.

The girls decided that it was important to get to the bottom of the mystery. If mom had to stay in that house again, they had to be absolutely sure that it was safe.

A police complaint had been filed, but obviously, no action had been taken on it.

Now, as Anika took care of mom, Mihika took two months off from work and came to live in her mother's house. Every morning, like clockwork, she would reach the police station. In a week, she convinced someone to at least see the CCTV footage from the public cameras near the street. They did not find anything strange or different in that. The usual – drunk people falling on the street, two-wheeler daredevilry, delivery boys, late night cars, some social visits. No suspicious vehicles or people.

Finally, Meena, one of the lady constables, started taking an interest in her. One day, over chai, Mihika told Meena why she needed the house to be secure before her mother returned to live alone. This was not just a case of pursuing a failed crime. It was a case of preventing a future crime. Aunty had been right. If a crime happened in an old building like theirs, it was very likely someone who knew her mother. Or, at least knew that she was an easy target living alone.

It was this line that Meena caught on to, "Yes, you are right. Someone knew she was an old lady living alone and could be attacked. The first angle we check in these cases is property disputes, family disputes, relatives, and old business associations. Any enmity or even a small dispute that you can think of? I don't have the time to follow all your leads, but if there is something that is promising, I will try and speak to my sir."

Mihika could not think of anything off the top of her head. She came back to do some homework. Anika, mom, and Mihika got on a call to brainstorm and think of everyone who could want to hurt them. She also spoke to the neighbours and the sole building guard to ask if anyone was seen lurking at the building in the weeks before the assault. Since the theft attempt, the guard was visibly shaken and the overall security at the building had gone up. There was also talk of installing CCTV cameras and paying the salary of a new night guard. The building mostly housed senior citizens living either alone or with families. Some residents thought that cameras did a better job of security than night guards who would anyway sleep on duty. No night guard has ever been found awake all night. That is where the decision was stuck.

For all their hard work, the sisters drew naught. No one was seen lurking near the building. The guard or the neighbours had not noticed anything. No relatives or old friends had suddenly visited mom recently. No phone calls even. Nothing at all.

Mihika reported back to Meena. Meena thought for a while and then asked, "Where does your mom keep her money? In the house? Or in a locker? Also, has your mother recently bought any expensive item or jewellery?"

"No, but Anika and I gifted her a chain and a pendant this summer. She had started wearing that."

"Was it big?"

"Reasonably big, yes."

"What all jewellery does your mother wear on a day-to-day basis?"

"Four gold bangles, this chain, her earrings, five rings, and I think.. that's it."

Meena did a quick calculation, "That is approximately worth three lakh rupees in jewellery. Thefts have happened for less. I think we can proceed with the theft theory. Where did you girls buy the jewellery? We can start with staff from there."

"Anika bought it from her city. No one here."

"OK, Mihika, I will take out the phone numbers that were active in your building approximately, at the time of the theft. It is tough, but I think that three lakhs' worth of jewellery and a human life might convince my boss."

"Should I also add some paper money?" Mihika asked, hesitantly. She had been coming to the police station regularly and knew that paper money was the term used at this station to indicate a bribe.

Meena smiled, "Relax, Mihika. Some police folks are corrupt. But most of us put in twelve-hour workdays without expecting anything more than our salaries and respect. Instead of paper money, give me real respect."

Mihika apologized. Meena smiled. Then, Mihika went back to the waiting area of the police station. Even if nothing was expected, she wanted to stay visible.

Being in that waiting room was an experience Mihika never thought she would have. As the younger one, she had always been protected and patronised. Even now, Anika had taken up the main task of taking care of mom while she was relegated to this. But what an adventure it was turning out to be!

It is one thing to sit with your mother in a comfortable room, with an attendant ready to do things, and quite another to share a room with suspected convicts, rapists, and victims of crime who, quite often, just gazed into space, being there, like her. What she found most uncomfortable were the stares. They ALL stared at her – the police folk, the complainants, the victims, and the convicts. They all stared. Sometimes, women tried to start a conversation with her. Sometimes, the men tried to sit too close. This was a trauma that she was not going to get over in a hurry. And yet, doggedly, each day, she came and sat.

Two days later, Meena called her to her desk. "The phones in that location are here. You understand that our information is approximate only. These phones were in the area. They could have been in the next building also. Just go through this list. Anything that stands out?"

Mihika ran through the list diligently. Every number was checked against the number of everyone in the contact list of all three – Mom, Anika, and Mihika.

Nothing came up. Numbers of neighbours, nearby stores, late night delivery boys. Nothing out of the ordinary.

***

On the 43rd day since the assault/theft, Mihika was approached by a young lady in the waiting area of the police station. "Didi, main aapse 2 minute baat kar sakti hoon[3]?"

Mihika sighed. This was going to be a request for free career counselling. The girl looked barely seventeen. Very likely, she was writing her Grade 12 exams and her parents were pressurising her to marry. Or, perhaps, her boyfriend was forcing to get married. In her days here, she had spoken to 5-7 girls who were going through this. Like those girls, this one was also neatly dressed.

"Aao, baitho...[4]" Mihika made some space for her.

"Didi... I have heard you talk to that madam about a theft in your house. What all did they take?"

Mihika sighed, "Nothing. A man was trying to enter when my mom heard the noise. She came to check what was going on. The boy was wearing a mask, so she could not identify him. He attacked her, she fought back and started screaming. At that point, he ran away. But my mother had injuries on her head and face, a leg injury, and a broken arm. Long recovery."

"Didi[5]... can I please say something?"

"Haan...[6]" this conversation was not going the way Mihika expected.

"Didi, I have complained against my boyfriend. He hit me. I am not going back to that man. Like you, I am also here to make sure they take action against him. But when we were together, I heard him and his friends talk. Did your mother order a lot of things from a local delivery store?"

"No, not from one store. She used an app that gave her whatever she wanted."

"Then, didi, please check if any of those boys was in your house that day. I think Meena madam has given you list of active phone numbers in that area. Us mein se, delivery boys ke number nikalo[7], and ask them what they were delivering that time of the day. But didi, please don't mention my name anywhere. I am here with an NGO madam. She will not like it."

Mihika stared at this young girl.

Then, as fast as she could, she made her way to Meena's desk.

Meena looked up, as if to dismiss the suggestion, but then, perhaps, decided to give it a shot.

Because of the time of night, there were only ten active numbers that belonged to delivery boys.

A constable took up the task of calling each one and asking which company they worked for on the day of the attack.

Then, Meena called the local manager of these apps and asked for the rosters of these boys on that night. "I will give you the roster, madam, but sometimes customer only gives wrong address or something, or asks for something extra and instead of being painful, the boys just rush to the warehouse and get it for the customer. That is not done through the app. So, this roster may not be accurate."

"Chalega[8]." Meena responded.

She then matched each boy to his delivery roster to ensure that he was in the area because of an order.

At the eighth name, she could not find a match. There was no delivery roster for the boy.

She called the app and asked, "You have a rider called R. Was he not delivering anything that night?"

The manager asked for a moment. Then he checked his records and replied, "Nahi ji[9], he was not on duty that morning. His duty only started at 2:00 PM."

Jackpot!!!

The boy was brought in for questioning.

After the relevant rigour of questioning, this is the story that emerged:

He saw this instant delivery app and instantly saw an opportunity. He would join a delivery app as a delivery boy. On his beat, he would identify a target. Then, he would quickly execute a theft and take whatever was possible. He never got caught because in a CCTV camera, a delivery boy at any time of night or day was usually not questioned. Every 3-4 months, he would move to a new area and pick up a new beat.

His modus operandi was very simple – look for customers who order often. Profile them. Best if they live alone. Find out the time that they sleep or travel. Best to steal something from the house when they travel. For senior citizens, just enter when they are sleeping, take their day jewellery and things lying around, and leave. 15 minutes end to end. Working professionals who live alone and senior citizens – both don't bother with going to the police. He had never been caught because no one had had the time to go to the police station and complain. But he knew that even if someone did go to the police, a small theft would not feature very high on the police priority list.

Even this time, he was not particularly scared. He knew that the old woman lived alone, so there was nothing to worry about.

"How much money have you made?"

"In the last one and a half years, about 50 lakhs or so."

"Were you never scared of getting arrested?" Meena was incredulous.

"I stole just enough to stay below your interest level." R replied, almost smugly.

***

Anika still kept mom for another two months. During this time, the building invested in CCTV cameras of high resolution and also put in place some simple protocols for security.

Both Mihika and Anika were not sure if mom should live alone in the same house, but mom was very sure that she could not be anywhere else.   "My friends have missed me enough as it is. It is time to go back to the rummy club. Life does not stop with a crime."

****

[1] It is considered good business practice to answer a phone within three rings at a business.

[2] Bachcha – term of endearment. Literally means 'child'.

[3] Can I please talk to you for two minutes?

[4] Come, sit.

[5] Didi – a respectful way to address an older lady. Literally means, elder sister.

[6] Yes...

[7] From that, extract the numbers of the delivery boys

[8] Works.

[9] No ma'm

Epilogue

Hope you enjoyed the stories. Will you please take a minute to share your feedback?

Please review the book on Amazon, or, better still, please write to me directly!

Email: authnidhi@gmail.com

And, Let's Connect!

Instagram: @authnidhi

About the Author

Nidhi is an IT advisor. She is an MBA by education, reader by inclination, start-up founder by vocation, and parent by disposition.

The use of AI in crime and crime prevention is her recent area of interest.

This is her third book.

The first book, **Probe8** – a collection of eight short stories of modern crime, was listed at Barnes and Noble, Dymocks (Australia), Foyles (UK), Saxo.com (Denmark), and other international bookstores.

The second book, **The Small but Ultimate Book of Online Safety**, is an Amazon #1 Bestseller. The book is the smallest, most direct book of advice on how to stay safe online.